I0690622

GENESIS
AND THE SECRET OF EDEN

ANYTHING IS POSSIBLE IN THE GARDEN OF GOD

FRAN LYNGHAUG
Award winning author
of equine books and Christian novels

We Believe In The Power Of Authors

PO Box 221974 Anchorage, Alaska 99522-1974
books@publicationconsultants.com—www.publicationconsultants.com

ISBN 978-1-63747-093-0
eISBN: 978-1-63747-094-7

Library of Congress Catalog Card Number: 2022936403

Copyright 2022 Fran Lynghaug
—First Edition—

All rights reserved, including the right of
reproduction in any form, or by any mechanical
or electronic means including photocopying or
recording, or by any information storage or
retrieval system, in whole or in part in any
form, and in any case not without the
written permission of the author and publisher.

Manufactured in the United States of America.

ACKNOWLEDGEMENTS

I thank the following friends who helped considerably with the making of this book. I couldn't have done it without them! Skyla Hays for proof reading.
Karen King for insightful story line suggestions and proofreading.
Rev. Josh Mannon, Associate Pastor at Wilson Assembly of God, Wisconsin, for consultation on Biblical content.
Sue Schedin for editing and proofreading.
Char Svobodny for proofreading and textual suggestions.
Abigail Wild-Baia for her professional editing, proof reading, and story suggestions.
I thank my family who supported and encouraged me: My kids: Amee, Rick, Cat, and Josh, but especially my husband Dick, whose support meant so much. I thank God for him.
Most of all I thank my Heavenly Father who spoke to me often while writing this book. I consider this to be His work!

TABLE OF CONTENTS

I. Eve   1
2. Adam   7
3. An Unholy Place   13
4. The Spirit   20
5. Satan   26
6. Father God   31
7. Creator God   38
8. The Angel   49
9. A Walk in The Park   55
10. Living As One   62
11. Lucifer   69
12. The Tree   76
13. The Test   81
14. The Curse   86
15. In the Throne Room   92
16. Justice   98
17. Consequences   106
18. Hope   113
19. The Plan   119

20. Aftermath   125

Footnotes   138

<u>To the reader:</u> This book contains many footnote references from Bible scriptures. Footnotes are at the back of the book.

In the beginning, God created the heavens and the earth ...

Genesis 1:1

Then He made Man.

Eons ago in a foregone age, there was a mystical garden called Eden. The first man and woman created by God lived there, named Adam and Eve ...

I. EVE

Gentle, intuitive, intelligent, and curious.
Every movement a language of femininity.
A gatherer cherishing life of every kind.
Reaching out to embrace all to her bosom.
Unparalleled inner strength belying her daintiness.
Sparkling purity and innocence.
Fair as the morning.
Able to overwhelm the heart with one look of
her eyes.
Nothing can compare to her.
She is Woman
and she ravishes My heart. [1]

A slinky black creature crouched behind thick ferns and peered silently at a woman's figure as she bent over laurel shrubs a distance away. The fern labyrinth hid him well and he peeked at her between its leaves from his vantage point higher on an embankment. He folded his leathery wings tightly against his sides and followed her every move with squinted eyes. He hated the sight of her, but sank lower on scaly limbs to better hide himself.

The woman was swathed in light as she peered down at a bird's nest while a finch flew about her head. It was obvious she and the bird were communicating with each other and it caused the lurking spy to quietly scoff at them. He knew the woman was talking with her thoughts to the bird, but he had no understanding of her words like the finch did. The joy of the woman and bird were apparent, but they were oblivious of him.

His sullen countenance contrasted sharply to the peaceful little scene and he felt the difference immensely. He was well aware that he was the only creature hiding in all of Eden.

He glared at the woman with hatred and disgust. After all, she was infringing into territory that had been usurped. It didn't matter if it was done covertly.

Though she wasn't cognizant of the stranger watching her, Eve felt something out of place in the atmosphere and it made her uncomfortable. But it wasn't close enough to discern exactly what it was, so she disregarded it when the mother finch flitted about and chirped a robust greeting.

As she bent to part the branches to get a closer look at the clutch of baby birds, strands of auburn hair fell across her ivory white face. A glowing halo completely covered her entire body and illuminated the surrounding bushes, falling on the peeping infants within.

The nest was intricate and unabashedly exposed for all to see; there was no need to hide them or any young in all of Eden. She smiled and spoke to the infants with her thoughts. "You precious babies! Father will be so happy!" The mother finch swooped to a branch and cocked an eye on her. It understood her thoughts completely and flitted with ease, trilling a song, "Hap-hap-happy to see Eve!"

Songs from other birds as well as soft music from the surrounding flora filled the air, drawing her into their cheerful world. Angelic choruses above the clouds also drifted down, and when she disregarded the uneasy feeling, it was replaced with a surge of bubbling joy.

She could feel the presence of Father all around her. His smell was like rain after a storm, fresh and clean, and His warmth enveloped her. With her thoughts, she spoke to Him. "New life, Father! Aren't they beautiful?"

"Yes. New life is always beautiful." He was like a vapor, bending beside her and gently smiling on the spunky mother, who twittered and strutted up and down the leafy branch. "Hap-hap-happy to see the Lord God of all!"

He laughed with amusement, enjoying the birds just as much as Eve. [2] She relished this moment of mutual enjoyment and stood to twirl a joyful little dance with her arms extended out as if to touch Him in the air. Her light grew brighter, flickering like a candle while the mother tweeted around her head until He laughed again. [3]

High on the hill, the dark creature crouching behind the branches observed her and scowled in envy. He suspected her happiness was due to an interaction with God and he abhorred it. Anyway, this was the wrong time for a confrontation and he must report to his master what he had seen at once. Only too well he knew how it would be received and he scuttled quickly away.

Eve wasn't conscious of the onlooker's movement in the distance—she was having such a glorious time with God. *"Your joy pleases Me, My daughter!"* There was no reference to the creature He knew had just left. It would mar her joy and the brooding spy was of no consequence just now.

Eve paused, and with all seriousness, extended her hand over the ground, speaking boldly now. "Earth, produce abundant nourishment right here so my mama bird won't have to go far to feed her little ones."

Her distinctive blue eyes were stern and her voice held much authority, causing the ground beneath her feet to react.

It had life of its own deep inside and it responded to her command. [4] It heaved up for an instant, as if swelling to release its bountiful supply, then reclined back into place. The lush green grass and branch hands of the palm trees sprang to attention. Though hunger was virtually unknown, she could feel Father's approval.

Gazing at the nest with its babies, she couldn't help sighing, "Oh, how I yearn to mother a baby just like animals care for their little ones!" She laughed a little in anticipation of one day cradling her own baby and God laughed with her. He wanted her to have babies too.

"When will I have a baby?" she asked Him. "It has been so long since I asked for my own child. How I wish for the day I can hold my own baby in my arms!"

"Later," He said, *"at the end of the day I will speak to you about it."* His reassuring words overwhelmed her and her spirit surged with happiness.

Then, in the next moment, she did a remarkable thing. She lifted into the air with just a thought—her will alone—without benefit of any earthly appendage! Quick as a flick of light, she moved instantly and effortlessly into the sky. Like the angels, she soared through the air faster than any other physical being. [5] Flight was easy for her and she expressed her delight with laughter as she swooped through the air.

If she had looked back, she might have seen the dark stranger moving away in the opposite direction, but her attention was elsewhere. She sped over the treetops that dotted the green carpet of Eden's lush landscape, then lifted higher into the blue morning sky.

Sunshine pushed aside a gentle mist covering the earth beneath and its warmth pushed the heady scent of greenery upward to welcome her. She skirted the area with its verdant fields laden with grain stalks swaying gently in the morning breeze and its heavily scented fruit trees wafting their aroma up from the hills and valleys.

The further she went, the easier it was to disregard her apprehension that something wasn't quite right. The day was too glorious to waste on anything disturbing.

She passed over a lazy herd of cows grazing in a meadow as a brightly spotted leopard yawned and stepped out in the open, surveying the landscape. Its interest in the bovines was casual, nothing more than a passing glance. Behind was its family of older cubs gleaning on succulent vegetation. [6] A herd of horses also meandered on a vibrantly green hillside and flocks of colorful birds filled the sky. She knew the thoughts of the leopards instantly as well as the cows, horses, and birds. Her connection to them was clear, uncomplicated, and instantaneous. All was in order, as it should be.

Angelic songs floated in the air from an ethereal distance away and swelled to a high crescendo, so she sang along with it. [7] Birds of all kinds and descriptions also sang harmonious songs along with the angels, filling the morning breeze with happiness.

As she tuned to the singing and the energy around her— the grandeur of the landscape, the grazing creatures below, and the trees swelling with uplifted branches—it overwhelmed her.

How very natural it was to sing to Him! "How wonderful to have God as my Father!" she sang. "He is always with me and makes His animals just for me!" She felt part of the living orchestra playing out in the land beneath her as she swooped by.

She mounted higher, glorying in her flight of freedom. Just below the lowest clouds, she passed four stream beds until they merged into two main rivers almost parallel to each other—one would later be known as the Euphrates River, the other the Tigris River. These river heads marked the outskirts of Eden and she banked above one of the powerful waterfalls along the Euphrates as it gushed its song.

She skirted over the river, tracing its backwaters to a lush delta, and laughed as the wind tickled through her hair. Flowers were everywhere, dripping with dew. Their aroma

5

fanned the air with intoxicating perfume as they sang and raised their faces up toward her.

A majestic mountain framed by white clouds loomed ahead with a spattering of agile mountain sheep scaling its side. A family of bears lolled beneath it, indifferent to the action of the goats, and an eagle soared in the distance, gathering the currents of the wind in its pinions.

She passed them by and approached the glittering towers of a palace—home! It was a magnificent structure standing boldly apart from the surrounding mountain flora with elegant turrets and graceful archways and a pair of stately gates standing open and welcoming. Its brilliantly jeweled walls and agate towers gleaming in the sun never failed to impress her. (8) The glittering walls of the courtyard encompassed a large group of angels robed in white. They milled about, singing while they waited in attendance.

She bypassed them, alighted on a balcony, and strode into a spacious room that glinted with contrasting sapphires and topaz gems in the walls and high arched ceilings. The floor was a type of transparent gold, thick and cool beneath her feet. (9) Even the gems in the walls, ceiling, and floors were singing their quiet melodies. (10)

The room contained very little furniture and ornaments, but nonetheless was elegant and pleasing to her. Adam had built this aesthetic mansion long ago and she was proud of his handiwork. An elaborately ornate wood table overlaid in gold along with four gem studded chairs stood in the center of the room. Adam was bent over a map laid out on the table with two huge angels beside him and she was excited to tell him what God had said.

At that very moment on the far end of Eden, the dark creature also dove through the sky and zoomed past the clouds on his way to a barren land in the distance.

He needed to report at once!

II. Adam

Man ...
Strength with patience. Courage with fortitude.
Honorable and faithful. Stalwart and capable.
A force to be reckoned with.
Masculine in all attributes, yet with considerable kindness.
A suitable companion who pursues after Me.
Mirroring My power and compassion like a driving storm.
Formidable, yet in complete control. His authority second only to Mine.
He is the expression of My heart.
I desire to guide him, teach him, protect him.
He is My beloved son,
And I am very pleased with him.

Adam mused over the map spread out before him. Like Eve, he was robed in a dazzling and constant eddy of white light that blurred his outline and enhanced, rather than hindered his air of authority. [1] However, it didn't completely hide his black, kinky hair and reddish bronze skin. [2] His deep brown eyes, starkly opposite Eve's sparkling blue set, seemed perplexed at the moment as he pondered the map.

He was focused on a particular area in Eden and seemed overly concerned about it. He sensed something wasn't quite right there. He could feel it.

The two angel figures huddling beside him were also intent on the map and obviously shared his concern. Like all the angels, they were different from Eve and Adam. Though they glowed with the same white light and their faces shone like lightening, they had a pair of overlapping wings folded neatly on their backs. The wings were as gleaming white as their linen mantles and curved from above their heads down to their ankles. Their mantles were smooth and sleek without a spot or stitching of any kind. [3] Light curly hair tumbled about their shoulders.

As the two straightened, their enormous height and breadth seemed to fill half the room. They towered head and shoulders over Adam at nine feet tall. Each had broad shoulders and emitted a noticeable power similar to soldiers. Yet their faces belied their peace and serenity with broad smiles as if they didn't belong on these bodies, even as they concentrated on the map.

Though Eve approached silently by gliding across the cool floor, all three turned as one, instantly aware of her. As their beams of light united, they looked as if they were on fire.

They respectfully acknowledged her entrance in a most extraordinary way. Their thoughts and impressions darted into each other's minds where they were acknowledged and answered by all simultaneously without a sound being uttered. Though they spoke without precise words, the personality and intent of each was interjected in such a way that their messages were clearly understood by all. [4]

"Good morning to you, Eve! We see you have been walking through Eden and we invite you to join us."

"Ah, Adam and good Raphael and Uriel! What a glorious morning this is! Can we share it together?"

Distracted for a moment from the map, Adam gazed at Eve and a grin filled his face. She was flushed with exuberance from her morning outing and it highlighted her natural loveliness. The sight of her struck him with a sudden urge to draw her to his side and cover her with a protective arm, which surprised him because it didn't make sense. There was nothing dangerous in Eden, but an inner desire to cover her with his strength was particularly intense today for some reason.

"How strange," he thought, "that on this morning I feel it so strongly!"

His thoughts weren't hidden from Eve and she also found them a bit surprising, since Adam had been so focused on the map. It flustered her a bit at his gallant attitude and she glowed with a responding smile spreading across her face.

The two angelic companions were also aware of his thoughts, but didn't turn discreetly away at the interaction between the two. Instead, they beamed knowing smiles.

Eve flowed to Adam's side as he returned to the map. She spoke to him with her thoughts. "What is it you are working on?"

He responded with his own thoughts. "That section south of here has become barren with swamps surrounding it and it's out of balance." The swamps bothered him more than they should as he pointed them out with growing consternation. "We are thinking of redirecting its swamps off into streams or waterfalls deeper in the land. Something needs to be done with it." Then he added, "Soon. It is now overrun by reptiles and other amphibians, big and small. It is too fetid to produce much else."

He knew every species of animal and reptiles were just as much a part of Eden as any other animal, but barren land in the midst of swamps was glaringly out of place, especially in

Eden where only fertile, pleasant land took precedence. He also sensed an unusual quickening in his spirit that something else was wrong about this particular area, but he couldn't detect what it was. "We know there is a wilderness beyond Eden," he continued," but this is within Eden."

Eve interrupted. "Adam?"

"Hmm. Yes?"

"I saw a nest with new baby finches this morning!"

He knew where this was leading but continued his focus on the map. "I know your desire to have children. I want to have them too. Father said we would have them. Your wants are my wants. We must be patient."

She was excited to tell him, "Father promised to talk to me later about it. We might have a baby soon, don't you think?"

"Only Father knows the time. For now, I would like to make some changes in Eden before we have our first child. There is so much I want to do before then."

Abruptly her countenance fell and he became aware of her dissatisfaction. It was so strong that it pulled him away from the map. He turned and scrutinized her for a moment to consider his words before speaking. Taking her hand, he sat beside the table, and pulled her down next to him. "I know you want babies right away and I do too. But we can get ready while we wait."

Rafael and Uriel sat with them and Raphael reminded them, "God has proclaimed that you are the beginning of all peoples on the earth." Uriel interjected, "His word is true and binding. You will have children!" His statement was so strong that there was no questioning the accuracy of it.

Eve sighed with impatience, so Adam gently reminded her, "We have spoken of this before. As our children grow to adulthood, Father wants each of them living in a portion of Eden that is perfect for them and close to us with their families. I want them always close to us too, but they should each have their own kingdoms."

"But it's taking so long!", she replied.

Adam paused to think on this before responding. "I was the only human for what seemed like a long time too before you came, Eve. It's not the easiest thing to be alone, even with angels and Father. He provided me with animals for companionship, and I appreciated them, but it wasn't the same." [5]

He spoke his thoughts while looking into her eyes. "I want family gatherings with lots of children sitting around our table and all the great times of raising children. I want a family just like you and I want them always close by. But I have learned to be patient for what is important."

She sighed. "It's just hard to wait."

"I know. I waited a long time too until Father put me in a deep sleep and made you from a bone in my flesh," he reminded her. [6] "You were worth the wait! Now we have Eden to care about."

Adam's thoughts returned to the map and this time Eve noticed his eyebrows scrunched together in deep thought as he stood to exam it. Rafael and Uriel joined him and they perused over the map together again, discussing it.

It wasn't often that Adam was this focused on managing one part of Eden and she felt the importance of his concern. "What is it?"

"This land on the outskirts of Eden, there's something unusual about it—it doesn't sit well with me." He rubbed his chin while he considered it. "Something is different. Why did it suddenly become swampy with the adjoining land a desert? It's out of sync and doesn't make sense. Raphael and Uriel have suspicions..."

He paused. He only recently knew the word, but to be suspicious was totally foreign to him.

Life in Eden was open and honest with an abundance of goodness that was given freely. All creation was the same with an overwhelming eagerness to give. For anything to withhold its helpful ability, be it plant, land, or animal, was so ... different. It was a perplexity to understand this.

Immediately Eve was intrigued with the problem. "I recognize the land you are pointing at. It's not far from where I was this morning. I did notice something different there, like it was out of place. I couldn't tell exactly what it was."

Her comment solidified his doubts and the four examined the map with renewed interest. Each opinion was respected and considered. At length Adam rolled it up with a decision. "I'll view the area myself." At once they all requested to accompany him.

Rather than walk across the floor, they skimmed over it and lifted off the balcony as one into the open air while continuing their discussion, then whisked quickly through the sky.

III. An Unholy Place

The four soared high above the ground, now laughing and reveling in the morning sunshine. Adam and Eve glided through the atmosphere just as easily as Raphael and Uriel. Their strong spiritual natures completely overpowered their physical bodies, enabling them the freedom of instant flight common to all spirits. Translating like this was as normal for them as breathing and they moved effortlessly together with the angels and quicker than any bird or insect. [1]

Raphael and Uriel's immense wings unfurled and arched over their backs, but their mode of transportation was identical to Adam's and Eve's. They simply passed through the atmosphere without benefit of any physical aid because they were spirits. Their wings didn't flap or otherwise move and were of no apparent significance other than adding to their overall beauty.

The wind was cool on Adam and Eve's faces, trickling through their hair, lifting it off the napes of their necks—it was fresh and invigorating. Far below, the earth swished by, tumbling with vibrant vegetation and its warm aroma wafted up to them. Birds of every size and color were awake and announcing that fact with clamorous singing. The dips of little valleys and foothills were vitally alive with stirring, yawning creatures, rising to the day. It was good to be alive!

Like dolphins playing in the sea, the four darted through the frothy clouds, flexing their powers—fading and appearing, rolling and plunging through the heavens. Eve laughed, dove, and surfaced again with giddiness. Adam grinned and faked chasing her along the way while the angels flanked them and participated now and then with their own antics. All thoroughly enjoyed the gaiety of the day.

They passed over the river heads and the area Eve had been to earlier until they drew near the swampland, then proceeded more slowly. They hovered over it and as they did, their mood quickly reversed. This was indeed a sober situation.

The swamps were murky and miserably ugly with wilted, damp vegetation and a distinctively foul smell they had never known before. Its putrid stench rose from brownish, stagnant mud, repulsing them. It was infested with small, slimy life forms wriggling around the dankness of the muddy edges. There were very few birds here.

The four were surprised and slowly passed by to proceed to the dry area. Here the land was acrid and barren of plants with minuscule type animals compared to the swampland. The ground was harder, caked with dry layers of sandstone, with cracked, jutting mounds—something in sharp contrast to Eden's lush elegance.

Adam lighted on the ground and studied it from a small foothill. Raphael and Uriel joined him, but were disconcerted and shifted uncomfortably with their thoughts racing between each other in concern. Eve, beside Adam, was curious.

Adam frowned. There was something else he couldn't comprehend about the place—something diverse and devoid in the area. It was blank with no response to him, almost recoiling from him. He was used to the life of the earth, as if it breathed on its own. It always responded to whatever he felt or commanded, but this land had no such expression.

He strode forward a short distance and the woman and angels fanned out from his side. It was a bleak wilderness in striking contrast to the adjoining swampland. They were all very quiet, the joy of minutes before now gone.

Suddenly Adam tripped and almost fell over something. On closer examination, it proved to be a young goat lying on its side and blending into a dull mound of dirt. It was cold and still and the eyes were unblinking with a sort of clouded film over them.

Adam and Eve bent over it, then stared at each other with bewilderment, probing each other's minds with questions, baffled. Adam poked the body but it was without energy. "A body without life—how strange! What function could this have?" he exclaimed. He was familiar with goats and this wasn't typical of any stage of growth.

Eve gasped a little in astonishment as the significance of the moment startled her. "I must be mistaken! I don't have any communication with the goat like I can with all animals! My thoughts to it are coming back blank!" Breathlessly she asked, "What can it mean?"

But Adam didn't answer; his thoughts were a jumble, a fact alone that was cause for alarm. He had never known confusion before. With determination, he sorted out the obvious facts and spoke out loud as if to explain them. "This is a goat. Goats don't lie on the ground with no energy or breath in them. This is not right. But I have authority over that. Animals always obey me. I will order it to move normally!"

He crouched closer over the goat and gently touched its shoulder. "Be full of vigor and eat, so your strength may return!" He waited a minute, but there was no sign of a responding movement. He had assumed wrong. The goat was not weak and he struggled to comprehend it.

Eve withdrew a little, startled. It was astounding that a command wasn't obeyed. It had never happened before! She didn't know fear, but she began to want to withdraw completely, all curiosity for the moment forgotten and anxiety taking its place.

The four remained silent with immobility and uncertainty. The angels stood a distance away on either side, scanning the immediate landscape as Adam and Eve examined the goat with consternation and perplexity. All was so still that the silence seemed to have a persona all its own, as if another being crushed them into a fixated state, defying them of all rational thinking or explanation.

A movement caught the corner of Eve's eye and Adam saw it too. It was no more than a shadow, a blur scurrying into a patch of wilted bracken. There was no time to react. One moment it was there, the next it was gone.

Eve shivered involuntarily and sidled next to Adam for assurance as he too scanned the area. She noticed his brow was furrowed and his lips were drawn down at the corners as he searched the spot where the shadow had retreated.

He was more than concerned now. This was a predicament he had never encountered before. The hair on the back of his neck prickled—a very strange sensation! His palms became sweaty and a rising warmth expanded up from his chest that made him glare around with a ferocity that was foreign to him.

In an instant the two angels were beside Adam and Eve, sensing their alarm and discerning trouble. Not a word was spoken. It all happened so quickly and now the stillness was palpable. The angels stood poised, all smiles and serenity of the morning now gone, and the power in their stance was bold and serious as they awaited a command.

Slowly Adam rose to his feet. His arm muscles were flexed and his jaw was set. He shouted openly for all to hear, "I am lord over all the land! My Almighty Father has given it to me! I am ruler here!" The light that engulfed his body fairly bristled.

It was a shout of declaration directed at the shadows, or the ground, or no one in particular, or everyone within earshot. But there was no response, just heavy silence, like a presence. Only the distant eerie braying of a jackass could be heard.

Eve wanted to move, to go home, but she couldn't. The foreboding on this dreary, hot ground was sinister and demanded attention. She felt a strong impression to be still, not to disturb it, as though it would expose her to something worse than the dead goat at her feet. Her chest was throbbing with a quickened beat that rang in her ears.

A cloudy fog rose abruptly out of the ground about fifty feet in front of them. A figure in its midst gradually took shape. There were other, smaller forms that appeared behind it and the somber hue of them brooded about, distorting the details of each.

From that distance the main figure looked like a magnificently handsome person with a cherub-type face, beautiful golden hair, and a flowing, glittery robe that sparkled like inlaid gems. He was bigger than Uriel and Raphael and exuded an intimidating power that had the effect of royalty, yet lacked the light that was typical of angels. Huge, sparkling wings were seated on his back.

His beauty was in stark contrast to the smaller, dark figures that crouched behind him while he glanced about as if looking for something. With resignation he faced the four and smiled pleasantly, but the words that came from him were foreign and garish in accent. He didn't send his thoughts to them the same way Adam and Eve talked with their thoughts, but used spoken verbiage.

"My greetings to you..."

That was as far as he got. Raphael and Uriel drew their swords from sheaths that were hidden in a fold of their tunics, readying for a charge. They obviously knew this person and

17

were bracing for battle. Their action took Adam by complete surprise. He didn't know they even carried swords!

Eve shot a quick question to him, but he stood transfixed, staring at the apparition without answering, which astonished her even more. Raphael and Uriel's thoughts were so angry she couldn't decipher them and it shocked her that they could be angry at all.

It was a baffling, surreal moment with no conversation between any of them, which had never happened before. For the first time, Eve experienced what it was like to be confused, vulnerable, and alone. A strange, tingling tenseness pulsated through her body and rang in her ears. It was unfamiliar and caused an additional and heightened alarm.

She didn't know what it was like to flee. She just knew she had to leave quickly. She lifted into the sky and when she had attained a good height she darted toward the palace. She couldn't think about this stranger to Eden or even consider him. She just wanted to be home immediately. She didn't even think about leaving Adam. The thought to get away fast was too overwhelming.

She was aware of someone at her side. It was Uriel. He didn't speak to her thoughts, but his expression was grim. The idea of protection never entered her mind as the reason for his escort. She was upset and it soothed her to know he was there. Together they sped silently toward the palace through the clouds they had just rollicked through, but now they took little notice as they streaked seriously on. The green panorama beneath streamed by, again bright and alive, but they paid no heed.

Eve's throat was strained and her mouth felt parched. Nevertheless, they continued to the glittering fortress, for surely it seemed like a fortress now. "I will drink there," she thought.

The gleaming walls of the courtyard loomed ahead. The walls weren't much taller than five feet and served more as a fence border than true fortress walls. Nevertheless, she was relieved to be there and slid through the open gates where the group of smiling white angels were gathered, singing. They stopped to acknowledged the two, but she turned and faced the gates and they swept shut in obedience with a clunk that was secure.

The angels parted for her and Uriel, startled by their hurried entrance and somber faces. They swept past them and Eve noticed it wasn't until then that Uriel settled his sword back in its sheath.

Her thirst was forgotten. She had only one thought. She would call Father to come right away!

IV. THE SPIRIT

The Lord possessed Me at the beginning of
His way,
Before His works of old.
I have been established from everlasting.

From the beginning, before there was ever
an earth,
When there were no depths, I was brought forth.
When there were no fountains abounding
with water,
Before the mountains were settled,
Before the hills, I was brought forth.
While as yet He had not made the earth or
the fields,
Or the primal dust of the world,
When He prepared the heavens, I was there.
When He drew a circle on the face of the deep,
When He established the clouds above,
When He strengthened the fountains of the deep,

When He assigned to the sea its limit so that the
waters would not transgress His command,
When He marked out the foundations of the earth,
Then I was beside Him as a master craftsman.

And I was daily His delight,
Rejoicing always before Him,
Rejoicing in His inhabited world.
And My delight was with the sons of men.

Proverbs 8:22-31. New King James

Adam remained in baffled silence while confronting the
stranger, but unaware of something else happening. The wind
picked up and there was a swishing sound as the Spirit of God's
holiness appeared overhead. He had a large, cloudy shape that
resembled Father God, but just for a moment. Culminating
clouds rolled about His form which moved and distorted His
image until two huge, outspread wings with feathery exten-
sions could be seen overshadowing Adam from high above.

The Spirit was poised in the center of the frothy wings
and He lingered there with His shadow covering Adam. He
strived to speak to Adam and give him wisdom in this time of
need. But Adam's full concentration was on the visage before
him and the Spirit couldn't penetrate Adam's will without his
consent. The most He could do was try to impress a foreboding
to warn him as he faced the foreigner.

Adam ignored Him and focused only on the angel, whose
evident superiority was clearly far above the angels Adam
was familiar with. He didn't seem to be human, but something beyond angelic, something with imperious authority
and power.

However, as the shapes behind the bright figure became
more distinct, they revealed dark, crouching beings that snick-
ered with a humor unfamiliar to Adam. They seemed more

aware than him about what was happening and they thought it absurdly funny.

Distracted with analyzing the group, Adam was unaware of another shadow, this one stretching from the towering stranger along the ground and seeping quietly toward him.

Slowly he stepped back toward Raphael and found it a relief that the mighty angel had a drawn sword. Not a word was spoken after the stranger's initial greeting. Now there was a disturbing stillness.

The Spirit waited for an invitation, an opening or question from Adam, ready to address the situation. Instead, Adam remained silent and perplexed. The link between he and God was stagnated, at least for the moment, and it thwarted the Spirit.

The golden-haired figure recognized the stillness as opportunity and addressed Adam. "My name is Satan. I am here to help you, your lordship."

Adam managed a reply. "Where do you come from and what do you mean by 'help'?"

Satan ignored the first part of Adam's question. "My only intent is to cultivate this wasteland into something more conducive to its potential beauty. I can easily transform it. Truly this is a waste of the land and we need to do something with it. My friends are also here to help us." [1] He motioned casually to the group of dark figures behind him while the shadow crept slowly onward toward Adam.

When did this being and his cohorts come to Eden and why are they here? Adam thought. I can't discern their life force like I can with every other creature. It is somehow masked from me. How bewildering!

The shadow was now expanding along the ground more directly toward him.

"Where do you come from and what do you mean 'help me'?" Adam repeated more directly and out loud. "Are you familiar with this wasteland? Why haven't I been aware of you before?"

Adam detected a small chuckle from the creatures behind the stranger which confused him more. He was unaccustomed to shrewd jealousy and couldn't detect the type of life residing either in Satan or the creatures. It was almost as disconcerting as the lifeless goat.

But Raphael definitely was not confused. He stood boldly facing the stranger, bracing against him with a force that was more military than anything else with his sword drawn.

The stranger simply ignored him. "Truly I come from the very throne of God." Somehow his smile was different than the smiles of other angels and his voice had a touch of sarcasm, but Adam didn't discern it. Satan continued, "I am sent to help you. I also have kingdoms to manage and know what it takes to get things in order for future generations. I am better equipped to help you than anyone else. That is why I am here."

It was fascinating to encounter such a creature as this! Never before was there anything like him and the idea of other kingdoms beyond the familiarity of Eden was a curiosity to Adam. The stranger was obviously a ruler, but he didn't look like a typical angel. As Adam grappled with the situation, he found himself irresistibly drawn to the possibility of advice from him. Did he know anything about the dead goat and why this land was so desolate?

Confused for the moment, Adam didn't notice the shadow was seeping ever nearer.

The Spirit was hovering closer too, impressing His force more strongly by the second. Adam flinched and then noticed for the first time that Eve had left. He was alone with Raphael and these creatures and he began to realize Raphael's stance was speaking louder than words.

Abruptly he comprehended a disadvantage, but the idea that there could be danger was foreign to him. Though he had never experienced it before, he slowly became aware of a threat, and he gathered his wits. "I am ruler over all this land!" he proclaimed again. "My Almighty Father has given it to me!" He was at a loss as what else to say, but the crouching creatures only chuckled more at his declaration. They thought it funny indeed!

The murky shadow extending out from them crept faster along the dry ground, stretching ever closer to Adam until it approached the fringes of the Spirit's shadow over Adam. It expanded to a dark cloud that began to surround him. Suddenly he felt overpowering dread and he finally opened himself to the Spirit.

In a flash the Spirit snatched him away and threw both he and Raphael into the clouds, then propelled them toward home without Adam thinking of it himself. Immediately he felt a sense of relief as well as guilt, but he didn't know why. Now all he could think was to get to Father and tell Him everything.

The Spirit blasted him and Raphael with a mighty wind quickly onward, urging them to make haste, and they streaked toward home. They couldn't get there fast enough! Not a word was spoken between them and it would have been confusing to form the thoughts and ominous foreboding they felt. The Spirit engulfed them with a fierce protective light as they blazed through the sky.

The jeweled palace seemed to loom ahead like a stronghold now. Strangely, the front gates were closed for the first time Adam could ever remember, but they swung open as the two alighted in the entryway. [2] It was a relief to hear the chorus of angels singing in the courtyard , but they stopped when they saw Adam and Raphael. They turned as one with astonishment as the two marched by with their faces set in stony walls of silence, just as they had with Eve and Uriel. There was no need to tell them they had experienced something disturbing.

Adam searched for Eve and found her with Uriel at the far end of the courtyard past the crowd of angels. Her face was aglow and turned upward and he knew she was requesting

Father to come. He gathered her in his arms and together they sent their request to Father.

For some reason, the Spirit urgently pressed them down and they bowed low while they waited for Father's arrival. This was also confusing and unusual because God always wanted them to stand while conversing face to face with Him, but it was impossible to stand.

They soon found His entrance this time was drastically different than any other time they had ever experienced.

V. SATAN

There was a party going on as a mass of Satan's followers danced around the dead goat burning on a fire. It was an offering of sorts, celebrating Satan, and as the goat burned with a putrid stench, they gleefully leaped around it. Though it had only been a minute when Adam confronted Satan, he had proven his inability to rely on God and handle the situation. They were ecstatic at his bungling conversation with Satan. They swarmed around the fire and shouted back and forth to each other with much boasting.

"All hail Satan! He will rule the earth forever!"

"He has captured the man and woman in their stupidity."

"The man in his stupidity and curiosity ..."

"... and the woman in her fear!"

"It will be their undoing!" was shouted with glee.

"Satan proclaimed it from the beginning ..."

"... when he took his leave from God!"

They bantered back and forth to each other and danced in jubilation. "God has allowed His 'pet project', His 'son', to do what he wills ..."

"... and it will be his undoing!"

"What a fool!"

"He's a spoiled brat!"

They smirked at Adam and Eve's response to Satan. "We have stolen God's pride and joy! We have stripped Him of His children! They are so gullible to listen to our master, Satan, the Schemer! We have found God's weakness and pricked Him in His eye! Lord Satan has outdone Him at His own game! All now belongs to us!"

They writhed in a distorted dance while gloom gathered from the dry brush surrounding them.

Draped in darkness and surrounding the outskirts of the fire with their sharp angled wings pointed down, they drooled and rolled with delight as they sneered their contempt for God as well as Adam and Eve. The foul odor of burning flesh filled the air, but their shouts of triumph only grew louder:

"So gullible! So gullible! Man is so gullible!
God Himself can't save him in his stupidity!"

They mimicked Adam when he stood confronting Satan, ridiculing him when he took a step back with a look of confusion on his dazed face. " 'I am lord over all the land!' ", they whined. " 'My Almighty Father has given it to me! I am ruler here!' " They laughed with derision.

"Stupid man! Stupid man! And his woman! What a cow! We will sacrifice her too and all her babies, if she can have them at all! We will stop the humans from increasing or make their children miserable. All the world is ours now!"

The fire smoldered until its dark smoke rose high in the sky. The embers cracked with heat like screams escaping from each dancing spit of flame. Steam from the goat's body swirled around them, then blended with the smoke and moved around the fire like a living thing. The demons excitedly responded with more leaps and shouts until they could hardly hear anything else.

Suddenly they stopped and stood waiting in a silence. Something was approaching from high above the fire, something that reeked of evil. It was a rolling, black cloud that descended from the sky. Sheets of flames escorted it down until it merged with the fire, igniting it with an explosion of sparks that licked the dry brush surrounding it. A fiery red figure rose from within it, shrouded by the smoke.

The worshippers resumed Satan's praises with renewed vigor as the figure expanded bigger and stronger until its shape transformed into a gruesome, lizard-like dragon. [1] It rose on thick legs and peered down at the worshipers, then threw its head back with roaring, mirthless laughter. Satan had arrived!

His huge red head had two twisted horns and a gaping mouth that opened in a grimacing smile. His yellow eyes glinted fiercely as he cackled and swept a powerfully long tail to encircle his fellow creatures, drawing them closer around the flaming offering. He answered them with his own smirks.

"Haven't I foretold it? Didn't I tell you? Man's folly will bring him down to hell!" Hatred for Adam spewed from him as hot as the flames. "His laughter will stop once and for all! When I'm done with him, he will be in everlasting torture. Maggots will spread under him and worms cover him."

He gloated in wicked delight. "But I will ascend to heaven and rule over all the angels! I will sit on the highest throne! I will preside on God's mountain over the congregated masses of angels on earth and ruling all of them up to the farthest reaches of heaven's northern boundaries! Yes, even in heaven!"

Pride poured out with his words. "I will climb to the highest heavens and be worshipped as the Most High." [2] He seemed to expand with his cleverness. "Man hasn't stopped me and I will overtake him easily! His kingdom is as good as mine now!"

He seethed with hatred for God and jealously of Adam. But his contempt for Eve was the vilest. "She's a puppet of Adam, doing his every bid, a dim-witted being with no merit of her own. I'll get Adam out of the way first, leaving her vulnerable."

Reveling in the thought of how easily he would cut and maim her, he gloated over his plan to pour such a depressing spirit on her that she would never be happy. "I'll wrack her brain with extreme suffering and stuff her mouth with obscenities instead of all that damned singing. I'll distort her feelings to the brink of suicide and then cause her body to ache with sickness."

Sneering his repulsion of her, he spat out the words. "She will never have babies! Mankind will end before it even begins!" [3] He spewed out hatred as he moved around the fire while hissing his remarks, as if he were already striking Eve with poisoned darts. In response, the demons danced with renewed energy, extolling his plan of destruction.

"I'll get Adam used to me until we are friends," Satan snarked. "He won't know it until it's too late. He's stupid to think he owns the world. He is weak. I'll take the earth from him easily! With him out of the way, the woman will do whatever I say, she is so gullible! She is just as weak as him and will blindly follow me instead of God. Oh, it is all so easy! God won't be able to rescue either of them because of His useless law. He proclaimed it Himself—the day they disobey, they will die! I, more than anyone else, know He can't go back on His word."

He gloated with malice and his followers cheered him on. "Gullible! So gullible she is!"

He sneered, "God has left Himself with no way out and I have overcome Him with my own superior intelligence! Together with my followers, I will destroy His world with perversions and evil. No one can stop me!"

At this he glared at the host around the fire, menacing them if they should think otherwise. They shrunk back a little in fear, yet his rash declarations drove them to total submission and greater frenzied worship. They knew he had the power to do what he said. [4]

He slithered down just beyond the embers and writhed with delight at the thought of stealing what God prized most—His children. His body coiled as if to strike and the tip of his tail flicked back and forth in anticipation. His eyes glowed with savage hatred and his fangs dripped with hot venom, salivating at the thought. He couldn't stop this glut for power, now that he had tasted it, and his thoughts to overtake God never wavered.

But a twinge of fear nagged deep at the root of his being. He knew more than anyone the power of God. Yet God Himself had bequeathed him with insurmountable strength and he wallowed in uncontrollable pride and rebellion because of it. How marvelous it was to stretch his boundaries beyond all restrictions!

"What He has done to me won't go unpunished! I will get back at Him many times over and He will pay dearly! I will stab Him right where it hurts the most, by snatching His damned 'children' right before His eyes." His own eyes shone with malevolence. "Revenge will be so sweet! I'll torture them, kill them, and take Adam's place over all God has created. Then I will take on God Himself right in front of everyone! The battle is just beginning!"

Smoke steamed out of his nostrils as he scoffed. [5] "Who is capable of stealing from God better than I? I'll teach Him not to mess with me! I'll have my day of vengeance! He'll pay a thousands of times over for what He did to me!"

His savage boldness inspired his followers. They knew his plan must not fail or the consequences of God's punishment on all of them was unavoidable. This had to work and they sallied with fists upraised. "We go forth together with you. God won't stand a chance. We pledge this to you! We will expand your kingdom—our kingdom—and bring more to worship you.

"The humans won't know it until it's too late!"

VI. Father God

My son, hear the instruction of your Father.

Proverbs 1:8. New King James

A heavy amber cloud descended just past the walls of Adam and Eve's palace courtyard, whirling as it fell. It roared as it billowed down, then hovered over the throng of angels who immediately sang a loud song of worship. Lightning flashed and hail swirled in the cloud as it furled and churned. The walls seemed to melt away, receding from its raw power as it spread across the courtyard. A trumpet blast sounded and reverberated off the walls and palace like the roar of a thousand lions. Father was coming!

Raphael, Uriel, and all the angels fell on their faces with deep reverence. The majesty of Almighty God expanded until it filled the entire area, engulfing Adam and Eve as well. As He descended, His authority overwhelmed them, and though they were bowed low, they collapsed completely and feebly before Him. It was impossible to do otherwise. The Spirit covered them with intense light, then stirred, and expanded that light toward the throne, melding as one with Him.

Father had come and He entered like never before!

Thunder sounded and a noise like tons of cascading waterfalls filled the courtyard until Adam and Eve shook at the force of it. [1] Then the power of His holiness expanded upward and out, filling the sky. It was a spectacle beyond human comprehension and far beyond anything Adam and Eve had ever experienced before.

The cloud surrounding God parted to reveal Him seated high above on a glittering blue sapphire throne so full of His tremendous brightness that it was impossible to withstand. He was immense, regal, and resplendent in a magnificent white raiment that was full of moving light. It trailed down the throne, filling the entire area. His face was so amazingly bright that it would seem to devour them and His hair blazed with strikingly white light shining out. Liquid fire encompassed His entire being so bright that it was almost impossible to view. [2]

Myriads of angels surged around His throne with joyous singing. They hemmed in the throne on all sides, dancing and singing exclamations, some with stringed musical instruments encased in gold. [3] More angels swooped out of the nimbus while announcing, "Holy, holy, holy is Almighty God!" They were completely overwhelmed in exuberance while singing the most beautiful song.

The only angels who were silent were two huge archangels who were much bigger than Uriel and Raphael. Adam and Eve knew them as Michael and Gabriel. [4] They stood reverently at attention on either side of the throne with their wings stretched out toward Him, which added to their appearance height. Their faces were radiant with startling light and their robes were dazzling white.

This was not at all what Adam and Eve had anticipated when they had requested Father to come. He had always appeared to them without much pomp whenever they wanted and welcomed their company. But this time His usual facile entrance had changed and His characteristic persona seemed to have changed as well, at least for now.

As He sat on His throne with brilliant beams radiating out, He observed Adam and Eve. He was terrifying in the beautiful ferocity of His holiness, and yet His love was tangible, pouring out and saturating them in soft waves. Disregarding the songs of worship, He focused only on one thing—His children.

He restrained Himself from comforting them, drawing them near, and embracing them, as any father would want to do. But before that could happen, He must establish that He was all powerful and they could trust and feel secure in His capability to protect them, no matter the situation. To display His mighty power was essential to their understanding of who He was in comparison to anything else that happened that day.

He turned first to Eve, giving her His undivided attention, for she was first to petition for help. His waves of soothing love settled on her. [5] *"Don't be frightened,"* He assured her. For a minute she was surprised, though she wasn't afraid of Him. His dramatic entrance had been unprecedented, but it was the morning's incident that had frightened her. Now in His mighty presence, all troubles vanished, and she almost had difficulty remembering the disturbing stranger.

He spoke into her soul, *"I have created you and formed you, My precious daughter. I planned everything about you and made you to have a place in My heart. No matter where you go, I will be with you. Nothing can hurt you as long as you are with Me."* Eve found herself blushing as she accepted His soothing words.

"I am the Lord your God, the Holy One, and you are most dear to Me. I love you with an everlasting love. Therefore, I will protect you." Then He cautioned her, *"But you must depend*

on Me and not be afraid. Also, I will bless your children. You shall surely blossom with children. You shall be a mother of many nations."

This last reference to something she briefly conversed with Him earlier in the day hadn't escaped His attention, although she had completely forgotten. At once she was reminded again that this was His desire too, to have many children.

She relaxed then and her elation returned. She rose to face Him and acknowledged His promise with a pleased grin and He smiled back. They shared a common desire, and united in this, they anticipated its fulfillment—the birth of her children. She felt very humble and was moved with gratitude toward Him.

"I am so happy, my Father! I am swelling with happiness inside! You know the desire of my heart and I am thankful for the children You will give me!!" She felt the Spirit surging approval alongside her.

Then God turned His attention to Adam, who remained prostrate before the throne. *"Oh, My son! How I long to teach you! I have given you a heart to guard and protect for a reason. Today was only the first time you have had to guard your kingdom.* (6) His words were earnest and Adam was taken aback in surprise. He knew God had commanded him to guard Eden, but he had never thought what it would entail.

"Listen, My son, to your father's instructions. If others entice you beyond My care, do not give in to them. They lie in wait to destroy you. Call upon Me in the time of trouble, My son, and I will deliver you." (7)

He leaned forward to emphasize His words. *"You are My first and only son and I made and established you on the earth with your own kingdom. I have given everything and every creature into your hand except for one thing.* (8) *There is nothing I want more than to bless you."*

Though the words were spoken with emphasis, they were surprisingly soft in explanation. *"I have given you authority over all that lives. Not only did I give it to you, but also to your descendants.* [9] *I breathed My own life into you, to call you My own son, separate from all other forms of life."*

After a brief pause, Adam stood to face Him before He added, *"As long as you belong to Me you will never need anything more. I am jealous of anything that tempts you away from Me!"* [10]

Then, more seriously, *"Why did you look upon the stranger and talk to him? Why did you not ask My counsel or consider the drawing of My Spirit?* [11] *There is none that can overtake you if you listen and follow Me."*

Adam recoiled as he thought of his hesitation with Satan and realized God certainly wanted to address it. He suddenly felt the seriousness of it—that his response at the time was weak, not at all like he had commanded other creatures in Eden. He had been easily misdirected during his confrontation with Satan and had, in fact, backed down and given Satan admittance without questioning it or asking the Spirit.

God knew his thoughts and responded. *"My son, listen to wisdom and hear My voice. Listen to Me and I will teach you to walk in My ways that you may stand strong and guard your heart as well as your kingdom. So I will bless you."*

He addressed them both now with a warning. *"If your heart turns away so that you do not hear, and you listen and obey another god, it would separate you from Me and you will surely die. Therefore, choose to follow Me that both you and your descendants may live."* [12]

Blazing streaks of light swirled around the throne as God proclaimed this. The two archangels, Gabriel and Michael, bowed on either side of the throne with their immense wings outstretched and with their faces down. [13] They awaited His command if He should give it.

Adam wasn't familiar with words such as this from his father and it surprised him. He had never heard Him say anything remotely close to a reprimand. Father always gave him whatever he desired. He realized there would be a cost from now on to being the only son of God.

Eve was also startled at His warning, especially after His generous words to her. When God had created them, He had given a similar warning, but they had known only acceptance and close kinship with their father, never an admonishment like this.

Of course, they would choose Him! Why would they listen to anyone else? Both were also perplexed at what "die" meant. Then the thought of the lifeless goat passed through their minds and suddenly they understood.

It seemed God expected a response, so Adam gave a single thought, an excuse that he somehow managed to convey through the Spirit with much trepidation. "Even if I were to lose everything, I would never forsake You." (14) He took Eve's hand and together they committed themselves to Him. It was a serious commitment—there would be no compromising.

"*I will always love and protect you both,*" God responded. "*Be honest with Me always and you shall receive grace and mercy.*" He stood up from His throne and indicated something beneath Him. It was a chamber with an inscription written on it: MERCY. Adam and Eve understood immediately that it was positioned there as the foundation of His love and care for them.

"*Later I will show you something I have waited a long time to show you. It is something I want you to see. You have a destiny to fulfill, a plan that is perfect for you, just as the plans I have for each one of My children who are not yet born. I will talk to you soon about it.*"

He gazed at them with a profound expression they had never seen before. At length He stepped down from the throne with His vesture trailing out and sweeping the steps. The angels fairly quivered with excitement, darting and flying about.

As He approached, Adam and Eve were overcome with emotion and began weeping. The events of the day had taken its toll as well as this bewildering conversation. He was God as well as Father to them and His mighty authority was overwhelming. His presence grew stronger the closer He came. It made them feel weak and they collapsed again.

He made a single slight movement with His hand and a shiver ran through them. They found themselves being lifted, yet no hands touched them, and they were placed gently on their feet closer to Him. Though they couldn't see any definite features in His face, they knew accurately His expression—it was full of compassion. He leaned forward and with His hand gently wiped the tears from their cheeks. [15]

Like any child wanting the comfort of his parent, they reached for Him and felt a tingling in their fingertips that strengthened them. It vibrated down their arms and entered their bodies, much like electricity. It was exciting! There was no one like their father!

Tenderly He scooped them into His powerful arms and they melted into His warm embrace in a poignant moment of love. [16] Regardless of what had happened before, they were one with Him now and nothing else mattered.

He whispered in their ears. *"I love you more than you can ever know."* [17] His beaming smile was so overpowering that there was no thought about His hint of something more to come. [18]

VII. Creator God

" ... ask the beasts, and they will teach you, and the birds ... and they will tell you, Or speak to the earth, and it will teach you, and the fish ... will explain to you. Who among these does not know that in the hand of the Lord ... is the life of every living thing, and the breath of all mankind?"

Job 12:7, 10. New King James

It was a week later when Adam woke in the palace's bedchamber as the dawn broke. A light breeze blew through the paneless window and a chorus of angels sang softly outside.

After that amazing day with Satan and then God, it seemed that all his strength had been drained away. Eve felt weakened too. They had done little since then except sleep intermittently, as if recuperating. Then Father had come to show them something else.

Adam stretched and yawned, trying not to disturb Eve who nestled beside him, but she stirred at his movement. He cradled her and pulled aside her auburn hair as he tenderly kissed her smooth shoulder. As pale as a bone, he thought. Bone of my bone, flesh of my flesh, so much a part of my life. [1] He reflected on what it was like before God created her. He had made Adam to mirror Himself with both male and female characteristics—the perfect combination of forthright-ness with tenderness—power with compassion. [2]

"I wasn't the only one without a mate," Adam mused. He was aware of some animals that lived a solitary life without much contact with others of the same species, but he held a unique status with God as a man, and he wanted something more—a counterpart to himself. "I loved you, Father, with all my heart," he addressed God, whom he knew was listening. "But You knew I shouldn't be alone. I'm grateful You made particular birds and animals just for me." [3]

He meditated a bit about that. Living with animals became second nature to him. They were his constant companions and he had a special bonding with some of his favorites. But there had to be more to life than living with animals. Then he thought about what God did next and how amazing it was when He presented Eve to him.

Eve stirred again and woke. She stretched, then propped herself up next to him. "Good morning! I'm surprised you aren't up already."

"I've been thinking about you," Adam said.

She snuggled next to him. "What about me?"

"I have been thinking what it was like before God made you. I am so glad He took a part of me to create you. You are perfect, far better than anything else Father ever made!"

"Yes, I remember when you told me I came from your side after He put you to sleep."

"I was surprised how small and delicate you looked com-pared to me. I don't know if I ever told you, but when I first saw you, you fascinated me. Because of you, I am happier than I ever was before!" He glowed a smile at her and fingered her hair. After a pause he said, "It would be difficult to live without you now."

"I know I came from you, but I'm glad I don't look the same as you, like some animal families all look and act the same. I'm different."

"I'm glad we are different too. I'm still fascinated with the way you move and do things. Just being with you makes me so happy. You understand the animals better than I do." After a pause he added, "I am surprised at how much beauty you bring to Eden too."

"Did you see the new flowers by the pond and the stone pathway that I made?" she asked.

"I would never think of doing something like that," he replied. "I was busy building a waterway and then a landfill. But you have transformed Eden with your charming ponds, little waterfalls, flowers, and stone paths."

He smiled at the thought of her personal touches. "I like to watch you when you're doing those things. When you touch them, they just seem to get more beautiful. Amazing! But I like it the best when you are at my side and we do things together. That is where you seem to belong, Eve. Father has fitted us together perfectly." Adam stopped because the love he felt for her was overwhelming.

"It makes me think about how God must have felt about me," he continued, "how much I brought Him happiness when I was created, just like the happiness you gave me. It makes me understand Father better and I'm grateful."

Eve thought about that for a moment. Then, "Remember the day we met Satan and Father came afterword to the court-yard? Satan terrified me! But when Father came it was a bit terrifying too!"

"I can't understand how we were able to be there, before all that power of Father", he replied. "The entire day was so strange. The dead goat, Satan, how our angels acted, but most of all, Father's reaction!"

They both lay there quietly pondering it. In the days that had followed that experience, they only spoke about it in reverent whispers to each other, mystified by it, until now. It seemed like it was all a dream, yet so profoundly real that it impacted them both immensely.

"Yeah, I had never seen Father's power like that before," Eve remarked. "If He didn't care for us so much, He could easily have crushed us! Yes, it was a strange day!"

"Do you remember what happened after that?" It was Father speaking to them. They heard Him so distinctly that there was no assuming what He said.

"Yes," replied Adam. "You took us to a mountain in the midst of Eden where two trees stood—the Tree of Life and the Tree of Knowledge of Good and Evil. (4) You talked to us about the trees and reminded us not to eat from the Tree of Knowledge of Good and Evil."

Eve added, "You also reminded us that we have access to everything else in Eden, including the Tree of Life. We know the trees are special."

"Remember I said you have all authority to manage everything and everyone and you can trust Me no matter what happens, but you must always be honest with Me."

"Then You took us on a journey and that was terrific!" Adam sat up and continued the conversation. It was as natural to have a talk like this with Father in the morning before doing anything else. "You whisked us high above the earth and we looked down on Eden from the heights of the sky."(5)

He thought about how Eden looked so pristine, like an oasis compared to other parts of the world. "We could see Your mountain in the center of Eden where Your two special trees stood and there were several other mountains close to it," he recalled. "A river divided the land and branched into four river heads as it flowed south. Two of them were almost parallel to each other and ran through the central part of Eden and the area around it."[6]

It was easy for Adam to be interested in the details of the land. This was his domain, after all, and it was good to see it laid out so it could be easily seen. He thought about expanding his map to include the entire area surrounding Eden after God had shown it to him.

He moved to the adjoining room where Uriel and Raphael waited respectfully before continuing. "We could see there was a large tract of land east of here that was part of an even larger land mass covering what we could see of the earth's surface. Where the four river heads divided south of Eden there were scattered swamps and we could see the boggy area on the outskirts of Eden where we met Satan."

Adam paused then with the uncomfortable thought of Satan as he sat at the table. Eve knew what he was thinking and sat with him, then quickly interjected, "Further on is a huge plain of grasslands combined with deserts and then there are rivers. Mountains are on Eden's west side and then there is more land and a lake."[7]

"A deep gorge is on Eden's east side," Adam added. "Mists and clouds covered most of the land so it was hard to see, but to the south there was a sea." [8]

Eve continued, "When we ascended to a higher elevation, we could see the earth was mostly blue with lacy white clouds and it was most beautiful! You brought us to the highest levels over the earth so we could see all that You had created and You explained about the heavens and earth."

She remembered they had no difficulty breathing or moving through the atmosphere because Father was with them. They were invigorated with His life spilling over and saturating them, totally engulfing their bodies.

Their thoughts about the trip seemed to blur after that because time seemed to stand still with the days merging together as they explored each heavenly creation.

"I wanted to guide you through the foundations of all I had made and show you their purpose," God said. Adam and Eve recalled how He relished sharing each creation with them, how they laughed together as they journeyed, and how He thoroughly enjoyed their simple observations and remarks. He reveled in their curiosity and encouraged it.

They had commented about each heavenly body and Adam and Eve asked questions about each new discovery. It strengthened and solidified their relationship with Father. He impressed on them how important it was to reverence Him above all creations by spending this time with Him and acknowledging His amazing power to create.

"I wanted to show you the secrets of life and the delight of all My spectacles:
How the stars stay their course throughout the heavens.
How each bright planet is set on its own route of passage.
The burning of the great sun in all its fiery magnitude.
How its rays break forth, diffusing its warmth over the earth in appointed divisions.
Where the course of the moon trails along her pathways in her revolving phases,
    and her growing and waning, set for signs of times and seasons.
The positions of the constellations at the ends of the earth and their circuits.
Solar flares and their traces through the galaxies.
How heavenly bodies and their trajectories render service to the earth.
How they are set forever in their casings, stations, and rulings bound by My law.
Times, orders, periods of dominion, and positions.

The coverings of the upper and lower heavens that surround the earth.
The chambers of the four winds: north, south, east, and west,
and how they proceed from their bulwark until they reach full strength according to their nature.
Also, their going forth and returning after discharging their vigor.
How thunder rolls out from its portals amid rumblings with lightning following on its heels.
How the canopy of clouds protects and replenishes the earth.
How the oceans are contained in their beds, but their waves are never at rest.
The division of each section of the earth and their set boundaries.
My magnificent mountain ranges and how they spew forth waterfalls.
How waters stream in the hollow of valleys and replenish plants each season.
Rolling grasslands with their carpets of green.
Snow and ice and where their moorings end.
Soft mists rising from the earth to water the ground.
Where the rain comes from and how the dew glistens with their bounty of refreshment.
The riotous seas and the creatures that live in them.
How angels measure out celestial boundaries with heavenly chords.
And the secrets of mercy and justice." [9]

Adam and Eve could hear Father as accurately as if He were there in the room and listened intently. They were impressed with the immensity of these heavenly and earthly realms and how everything adhered to God's will. The display of it all was just as fascinating as His mighty power to create such diverse and amazing stars and planets and how He protects the earth. But their greatest impression was how minuscule they were in comparison to His other creations. It was beyond comprehension of why He chose them as His most loved creations out of the vast expanse of the skies, heavens, and earth. [10] "It was a humbling experience," Adam admitted.

"My sustenance and commands radiate out from My heavenly residence in strands of My glory," God continued. *"They extend to all living things, worlds, and beings along these living cords, linking them to Me. My Spirit is the conduit, receiving My directions and relaying them along the same invisible lines.* [11] *He is a traversing agent, an extension Being coming from Me, and He pours out energy and direction to every creation. They complete the cycle of His directions in the same way— with their thoughts—talking to each other and connecting in a united way together. This is how I control all the heavens and the earth."* [12]

Adam and Eve were aware of this mode of transmitting thoughts between animals and knew of God's expressed guidance for each one. Every life had the ability to communicate with other life forms using the same silent speech. It was channeled freely and instantly through invisible "cords", as God called them, and received with perfect understanding and cooperation.

"This is how creatures interact with each other and their surroundings to survive," He explained. *"Use this wisdom to manage Eden. If a creature has no such cooperation or response to the Spirit—if it attacks another creature—it is a sign that it is not in communication and has to change or be expelled from Eden. It doesn't belong here."*

Father emphasized that this same interfacing connection— the language and knowledge of the Spirit—was consistently sent to Adam and Eve to call on whenever they were confused or threatened, as when they had confronted Satan. [13]

"Listen to the Spirit. For you have a destiny to fulfill here in Eden and even beyond that will include other lives." He reiterated again, "Listen to My Spirit. He extends these lines to unify everything and bring them into harmony with each other. None are left estranged or separated by themselves. Light, darkness, water, earth, space, luminaries, sky, plants, and animals—all have direction and purpose. All live in perfect harmony with other life forms."

Father directed both of them, "Be familiar with this plan of peaceful co-existence and take charge of anything in Eden that is out of place."

His message was clear. If there was a breakdown in this system, it could perpetrate misunderstanding, mistrust, or selfishness. "An animal is unconnected to the Spirit when it shows indifference, anger, or wildness, and it should be expelled because no creature should attack other creatures. (14) Claws and fangs are used only to climb or pick or eat."

Adam contemplated for a minute what "attack" would mean. "We have never seen an animal attacking another one. Why would they do that? It doesn't seem possible."

Uriel and Raphael shifted uncomfortably, but God ignored the comment and continued. "This intercommunication is necessary to sustain life so there will be no need for animals to die. It is My will for all creatures to live together like this, with no death."

He referred to angels next who had their own station and individual "bands"—their thought processes strung between themselves and God. "I created them to serve Me with joy and to accompany you and all your descendants wherever you go, but they are not to teach you. That is not what I created them to do. I am your only teacher. They belong to Me and receive My orders concerning you."

After a brief pause, He added, "Any spiritual being that doesn't have this tie to Me has alienated itself from Me and exists without My direction."

Adam and Eve acknowledged that their correspondence with God was especially strong. They knew exactly His words in their deep, innermost being—in their spirits—uniting them to Him in continual conversation. This form of speech projected not only Adam and Eve's thoughts to Him, but also their intentions and feelings that the Spirit routed back to the Father.

"Does all creation function together like this, by receiving the Spirit's direction?" Adam asked.

"Yes, it is for the common good of a thriving, healthy world," He replied. *"I know exactly everything about each creature and they in turn use the same speech pattern to communicate their thoughts to fellow creatures. It is to stimulate or revive a life wherever it is needed.*

Anything that doesn't have this connection to Me should either be corrected or expelled."

It was evident that there was more to managing Eden than what Adam and Eve initially thought. *"I planted Eden for you, but My will is for you to subdue the whole earth just like in Eden.* (15) *Eden is the beginning of My plan for mankind and My creations to populate the whole earth with My love and providence,"* Father explained. *"Teach your descendants how to care for this earth like you have done in Eden so My blessings will cover the entire world, and even beyond, when the time is right."*

It was an immense plan, but it gave purpose to their lives here and now, at the start of the human race, as well as the responsibility to carry it out. What would their children think if they should fail and creatures turned against each other and the happy interaction of all nature was destroyed?

"Most of all, teach your family how to follow Me by writing about it. My Spirit will inspire you what to write." Though Uriel and Raphael had been standing respectfully close by, they quietly produced a long scroll with a quill and placed them in front of Adam and Eve on the table. They showed them

47

how to write, which they found naturally easy to do. Father wanted them to record how He created everything and how He put them in charge of Eden. But most of all, they were to write about Him.

"What about that being we met, Satan?" Adam asked. "Where does he fit into all of this? Does he also have this capability to know the thoughts of others?"

"No, he does not. All he knows is what he sees. He is exempt from the privilege of knowing Me and the communication I have with My creations. He is able to send his thoughts, but he can't comprehend your thoughts. He only knows your thoughts or the thoughts of animals when he sees how they are behaving or when you talk out loud, not in your thoughts. Because he doesn't understand your thoughts, it angers him and he retaliates. I will speak more to you later about him. It is best to focus on Me for now."

Adam and Eve were satisfied and began recording all they had learned.

Then one day, a new visitor entered their lives with something more surprising still.

VIII. The Angel

Listen to Me, My people, My chosen ones ...
Come closer and listen. I have always told you
plainly what would happen, so that you could
clearly understand ... And now the Lord God
and His Spirit have sent me (with this message).

Isaiah 48: 12, 16. Living Bible

The sun had set and rose twice after Adam and Eve had journeyed with Father and when He counseled them about caring for Eden. They had been so caught up with Him that they had been unaware of passing time.

On the afternoon of the third day a special angel came to visit and invited them to walk with him in Eden. He was arrayed brilliantly in a white robe with a gold band around his chest. Though he didn't have wings and his height was comparable to theirs, he was so much like the mighty angels who were always there that Adam and Eve didn't question his presence.

He walked between them, lighting a path ahead. A small pageantry of angels, all in white, trailed behind and filled the air with their lilting melodies. Raphael and Uriel also walked with them, beaming their radiant smiles and singing harmony.

Walking now seemed like crawling compared to being whisked through the atmosphere with Father, but it had its own rewards. The sun shinned its warm hello and when a vast, startingly bright river was encountered, they drank deeply. It was crystal clear, almost like swirling glass. Its waters gushed a greeting to them with a titillating song.

The small party talked at length of the heavens and all the creations Father had shown them. The angel asked them what they thought Father's reason was to show it to them, other than to teach them about His creations.

While they considered the question, he answered for them. "It is so you understand that He has created all things and holds all eternity in His hands. He is deserving of the highest awe, respect, honor, and reverence, so you will keep His words.

"Everything He created has laws that govern their going out and coming in and He directs them. However, out of all His creations, you alone have a will to do as you please, except for one commandment He has given you—do not eat of the Tree of Knowledge of Good and Evil." His statement was another reminder to Adam and Eve about this tree and they acknowledged Father had already told them.

The angel continued, "But for you to have a free will, you must have His words in your heart. Otherwise, you would be out of control, just like the world would be without God's laws for them. Without keeping His words, you cannot know His will."

He gazed at them with a meltingly tender look in his eyes. "Father cherishes that you choose to love Him without any law except one, and that one is so you know He is Lord of all; it is for your good. [1] It is important that you know He is God over everything.

VIII. THE ANGEL

"He made you to have no kinship with evil and that is why you are forbidden to know or consider evil, even if it looks good. He loves you deeply." This last remark he spoke so softly it was almost a whisper. "But most of all, He wants you to know that He is capable of caring for you, no matter what happens, as long as you are honest with Him, abide by His words, and respect and trust Him."

At this, Adam and Eve realized that it was possible to hurt their Father by failing His purpose for them. This thought made them stop and think. They never considered that their Father, in all His mighty power, could be hurt by anything, but most of all that He could be hurt by them. It was amazing of the possibility He could be vulnerable.

The angel continued, "This is the Spirit of truth and knowledge—know Him, follow His words, and always believe and trust Him. Hear the Spirit of wisdom and understanding. He will instruct you and teach you prudence and discretion. (2) This is how your heavenly Father cares for you."

Though the angel was instructing them, his love seemed to flow out from his eyes and penetrate every fiber of their beings. "Father cares for you deeply and is worthy of all your love and trust. But He is a holy God and can't abide evil. If you should align yourself with it, it would separate you from Him, and separation from Him would be certain death."

He gave a deep sigh and with a troubled look he said very seriously, "You know about the two trees in Eden. One tree is the Tree of Life and the other is the Tree of Knowledge of Good and Evil, which is death to you. Your life existence depends on a tree, whichever you choose. To partake of evil, even combined with goodness, would be fatal. But if you keep His words, the Spirit will guide you."

Adam and Eve didn't need to be reminded again about the trees, but were bewildered at his warning. "We will always trust Father and do His will," they reassured the angel.

51

They stopped to eat then and discussed the meaning and significance of the angel's words of caution. Adam and Eve held each other and recommitted themselves to God. "We promise never to turn away from Him and always follow His Spirit." This was a more serious commitment than the one they had made previously because they knew more now.

The angel glowed his approval and a wonderfully deep satisfaction filled their hearts. The other angels retreated to the wayside when he produced a flaky white bread, dark red grape juice, and three silver goblets. They sat on the plush grass as he divided the bread and poured the juice into the goblets. As they ate and drank together in somber reflection, it seemed to seal the agreement between themselves and Father.[3]

The Spirit settled on them like a blanket, but with an intensity that almost took their breath away. *"I am burning into your souls the significance of this promise!"*, He said.

Father also spoke. *"I acknowledge your commitment and accept it with great gladness and blessings on you!"* It was a moment of mutual understanding and a bonding that was powerful, close, secure, and trusting between all of them. What joy it was to be elevated far above all Father's amazing creations and have this close connection to Him! What a privilege to look like Him, be with Him, and experience His overwhelming peace! [4]

The atmosphere was filled with His persona and joy flooded them. Even the air around them took on His fresh smell, like the aroma of flowers, heady and inviting.

The Spirit sang a cherry song then while Adam and Eve danced a jig together and laughed, throwing back their heads with total abandonment and freedom. [5] The angels joined in the gaiety and Raphael and Uriel were somewhat comical as they tried to imitate Adam and Eve's twirling. The other angel danced with them with great exuberance and they all danced and laughed together.

VIII. The Angel

As the day came to a close and the last rays of the sun shone brightly over the mountains, they quieted for a time of deep introspection and stood together in reverent silence as it set. The sunset's splendor glowed with marvelously soft mauves, striking golds, and iridescent blues that outlined the clouds and banked around the ray's edges. Clouds drifted lazily through the colors, churning them slowly until they sparkled like the facets of a diamond.

They immersed themselves in the beauty of it, slowly inhaling it, like inhaling God Himself. Deep appreciation and peace settled on them like one of the clouds as they stood in awe of its magnificence. They could never tire of God's creative craftsmanship and harmony in nature! How divine it was to be caught up in this life with Him!

They remembered His words to take time to be with Him and appreciate all He had made especially for them. It was so easy and inspiring to do!

The other angel smiled broadly at these thoughts, then rose up quickly into the sky until the clouds engulfed him out of sight.

"Let's spend the night right here instead of going home," Adam said. "I want to enjoy this as long as I can." He snuggled with Eve in the crook of a tree root as the night life hummed around them.

They talked briefly of their encounter with the angel and Adam mused openly about the look on his face when he spoke of the two trees in Eden. "Did you notice it?" he asked Eve. "His thoughts were hidden from me and it surprised me. I didn't get any of his thoughts at all! He seemed troubled about the trees."

"Yes," she replied, "but he was satisfied when we assured him we would always keep Father's will for us."

Adam thought about the angel's words as he pillowed Eve's head on his shoulder. The plush heath made a luxurious bed beneath them and it sang quietly as the warmly scented night air covered them and the angels receded in the distant shadows, singing softly. Adam whispered in her ear just before drowsiness carried them off, "Knowing our Father, how could anyone ever leave Him?" They slept the peaceful sleep of innocence.

God Himself, shrouded now in silent darkness, stood watch over them. Every part of them was precious, from the tips of their hair to the soles of their feet, but He treasured the purity of their hearts the most. He knew their innocence was not to last, but for now, He was content to be with them and protect them as their father.

His heart yearned to always be with them, talk to them, and hold them close, and more so since He knew what was soon to come. Then His thoughts were projected to future generations and how He would love them just as He loved Adam and Eve.

He sighed and engulfed them in His heavenly embrace as they slept. [6]

IX. A WALK IN THE PARK

The two woke to an amazing sunrise amplified by the sparkling of a nearby pristine stream with willows waving in the crisp breeze along its bed. Everything sparkled, right down to the soil along its banks. Being in love with God as well as each other made the world beautiful, invigorating, and right.

The park-like setting was dappled with light and the foliage of wildwood swaying in the breeze, seeming to beckon to them. So, they decided that another walk in the nearby vale was the best way to spend the day. Adam also wanted to survey anything needing improvement.

Again, walking seemed so mundane, especially after their celestial tour, but it was good to slow down and enjoy a more sedate stroll through the vibrant greenery of the garden. Raphael and Uriel followed along with a stream of white angels behind them.

Sunshine glinted off the woman's alabaster skin and the man's coppery limbs. As they walked along, the soft glow of their light enveloped them completely and outshone everything else. A more startling light beamed from their heads like haloed crowns.

They encountered a conglomeration of life along the way. Each sang a song that seemed to converge into one united voice, yet they came from a complex of personalities and natures. The bubbling of the stream over rocks, the warbling and chittering of birds, and the buzzing and blinking lights of insects welcomed them, but they had no trouble interpreting the speech of each. It was a marvelous conversation! The Spirit flowed back along the same lines with joy, charging each life with rejuvenating energy.

His care was evident in every creature they encountered and they marveled at each as they dawdled along. Soft melodies floated around in the surrounding little hills and valleys. The morning's breeze brushed the palm trees along the way, and they clapped their clustered branches together, waving them on. [1] Myriads of brightly colored flowers lifted their smiling faces and sang to them. Angels also trailed behind with their own harmonious songs.

Adam and Eve stopped by a row of waving trees dripping with succulent fruit and devoured their ripe juiciness. They snatched a handful of grain as it waved on golden stalks in the gentle wind and drank at the cool stream bank.

They almost felt sorry for the angels who couldn't relish the sweetness of ripe fruit or the crunchiness of grain; they never felt hunger like Adam and Eve did. It made the pair aware that all this abundance was only for those with physical bodies and they were grateful for it.

Every animal along the way responded to them with interest and without any trace of wildness or aggression. All animals were either grazers or browsers, only consuming fruit, grains, and herbs, but never any meat. [2] The death of a living animal was as bizarre as the death of an angel—it never happened. No animal was equipped to kill or eat flesh, as God had commanded. [3]

They strolled through acres of soft, intensely green grass and past a family of bears casually foraging. The bears ate with teeth that were more evenly shaped to crop bushes lining the stream and their paws were more like those of a dog.

A pride of lions lolled in the sun further ahead and a regal male with a full black mane separated himself from the others and approached them. His tawny body was huge, dwarfing Adam and Eve, and he carried himself with an air of stateliness. He was a special friend of Adam's and frequently accompanied him on his walks through Eden. Adam stroked his thick mane and immediately the huge feline's thoughts entered theirs: "My lords, may I accompany you today? My greatest desire is to be with you!" [4]

Adam responded, "Yes, please do join us, Baruch." As Adam's close companion, the huge lion was greatly respected among the other felines, but now he purred with the pleasure of a big cat as he strode majestically alongside Adam.

A herd of elegant horses of every color and shape grazed along the way. Eve sent a thought to one particularly striking white mare and immediately it turned and pranced to her. Eve loved this horse more than the others and she often rode her. She stroked her shiny coat, inhaling the mellow horse smell. Then she sank her fingers into the silky mane and hoisted herself easily onto the mare's back. "Good morning, Sky. Are you up for a ride?"

The mare frisked and bounced with enthusiasm. "Yes, let's GOOOOO!" and they galloped along the stream leaving Baruch and Adam behind.

Eve giggled with the surge of each powerful stride, reveling in Sky's strength beneath her. Together they fairly swept along the ground and Sky sang her song:

"Rushing, dashing, for the glee I taste!
May every stride with Eve make haste!"
I fly o'er field with silver stream.
Wind of the Spirit blow in my mane!

Thy life is flowing in my veins,
Dancing on the open plain!"

Eve reflected how wonderful it was when Father had shown them His spectacular heavenly bodies and intricate creations on earth. But the time she was spending now—casually walking in Eden with her husband, his lion, and riding her favorite mare—was also enjoyable, but in a different way.

She guided Sky to a walk and they circled around until they joined Adam and Baruch again. She dismounted and they all munched on rich greens along the way, which were sweet to the taste. Father had provided them with fruit, grains, and herbs for spices as well as grass and plants for animals. [5]

It was then that Adam brought up some thoughts that had recently come to mind, and the mood changed abruptly. "Did this world once have another ruler? Was there someone else before us?" he questioned. "The intruder we met before talked about other kingdoms and he seemed to know something about the dead goat that we didn't know."

His words cast a shadow on the day and Eve was surprised at this sudden reference to the strange encounter they had experienced with Satan. It was somehow forgotten when they were with Father. She stroked Sky next to her and toyed with her mane, running her fingers through it, as she considered Adam's thoughts about Satan.

For Eve, his questions seemed to border on debate by asking her to provide answers instead of asking the Spirit. It felt inappropriate and deep in her soul she felt a dullness. She was uncomfortable with it, but didn't know why. In all the world, they alone could inquire of God, so questioning each other about His plans for other kingdoms didn't seem quite right.

"God has only spoken to us about Eden and I think that is all we should be concerned about," she replied. "Do we need to know about other kingdoms?" She couldn't discern the truth behind the moodiness that came upon them now after such a glorious walk.

Adam shifted uncomfortably as the uneasiness settled on him too. It didn't enter his mind that there were no other kingdoms. He simply believed what the stranger said just as he had always believed what God said. Thankfully he turned his inquiry to Father, as he had been taught, and the Spirit was quick to answer. *"You speak rightly of him. He is an intruder and the truth is not in him."*

Adam was amazed and sat down in the fresh grass while contemplating this answer. He began to recognize that some of his thoughts were not from himself or God, but had come into his mind after he had conversed with Satan on that fateful day, though it was a very brief conversation. (6) Eve sat with him in the grass, trying to shake the gloominess that seemed to follow them now, while Sky grazed and Baruch lolled nearby.

Adam addressed the Spirit. "But knowledge is good. To me, it's exciting that there may be other ideas from another god-like creature like us. It was only the briefest conversation." He didn't realize he had opened himself to another point of view because of his desire to learn and identify facts, so he had taken in these thoughts unaware.

Immediately the Spirit responded with Father's warning. *"Remember all that I taught you and My words not to be deceived."*

Adam plucked a blade of grass and replied, "I am not deceived! I would never listen to this Satan! But I would like to know about other beings. Are there other intelligent life beings like Eve and I? I want only to learn what is useful and disregard the rest!"

"I have revealed to you much knowledge, but I don't want any knowledge of evil in you at this time. Everything that isn't good is evil. When I created everything on earth, I pronounced them good. Evil was never meant to be here. There will be a time when you will know more about evil, but not now."

Eve was aware of this conversation and was astounded at Adam's thoughts. But his next inquiry startled her more, especially after their talk with the angel. "Why must we have a command?", he asked, referring to God's command not to eat from the Tree of Knowledge of Good and Evil.

"My command is a boundary to your path in life and will help you learn restraint. It is only one command—do not partake of evil in any form, such as the Tree of Knowledge of Good and Evil. Because you are human, you must choose to obey, not like the animals or angels who live according to what I have determined for them."

Adam and Eve sat silently as they listened. They had never known boundaries before and weren't quite sure what it meant. Then they thought of the difference between Eden and the rest of the earth. Eden was luxurious compared to the lands just beyond it. God Himself had planted Eden and its beauty was different than the surrounding wildernesses. Crossing over to them was always a future intent, but Eden was too comfortable to consider leaving. There was no reason to go beyond its boundary. If there was a choice, they chose to stay and obey God.

"That is why you are so precious to Me, because you alone can freely choose," God continued. *"Your will is exceedingly important, both to you and Me. Because it is so important to us, Satan will try to steal it from you. To have your will in his control would make him ruler of the entire world. A command will cause you to use your will and decide goodness to prevail by involving Me. By heeding that one command, you choose Me."*

He paused for a moment to allow them to contemplate His words. *"The choice to trust Me enough to keep My words in your heart is your part in our relationship. My part is to freely give all I have to you without ever taking away your will. This is a binding acknowledgement we have with each other and it is precious to Me. I will never take away your ability to choose,"* then He added, *"no matter what happens."*

Adam was awed into silence as he listened intently with great respect for his father. He knew he had been gently corrected and presented with some consequences of failure to obey. He was uncertain what it would be like not to have a free will, but he valued God's will in his life. Meekly he determined to refrain from thinking of Satan, but for some reason, he didn't want to expel him from Eden.

The tiny germ of intrigue had taken root in his heart with the intent to ignore instead of act, "but just for now", he thought.

When all had been said and done, the fact remained that both Adam and Eve had the right to eject the evil one from their world. But neither regarded him as a threat, so the man ignored and the women hesitated with wonder. They didn't perceive what this would bring into their lives, and very soon.

X. Living As One

Adam straightened from the bulwark of drowned stumps and logs he was removing from the swampland on the perimeter of Eden. It was to provide a free flow of water to drain off some of the slimy muddiness there and the removal of debris was going well. Raphael was at his side, helping to relocate the soggy trees, which were lifted easily, no matter the weight. Adam had just as much supernatural strength as Raphael to lift or bend anything.

The logs were handily removed and repositioned to form an embankment along the side, but it was still a time-consuming project and it was humid here. The mud didn't stick to the two as they worked, but slid away, retreating from their brightness. They sang as they worked.

Adam glanced about in search of a place for the mud to drain off when he noticed something else on the horizon. It was a figure watching him.

"Greetings, Adam!" It was Satan.

###

Eve hummed to herself as she put the final touches on the cradle Adam had made. It must have the softest material for her first baby whom she was sure would come soon, as Father had promised. She straightened the downy bedding and surveyed the room with satisfaction. Smiling with Uriel at her side, she commented with a pleased grin. "There! Isn't it perfect?"

She had insisted the extra room with big windows be added to the palace so there would be a soft breeze blowing through when the days were hot. Viewing the billowy window sashes and baby covers she made sitting on the tableside gave her great happiness. She hoped it would be the boy Adam wanted.

Uriel smiled back. "It will be a beautiful baby!"

"I don't think I am pregnant just yet, but I'm sure I will be soon. Father promised." It was difficult for Eve to talk about anything else. The only disappointment that marred her day was Adam wasn't there to share the occasion.

"How I miss him! It seems he is spending more time with Raphael these days landscaping the terrain on Eden's outskirts." She knew he was revamping both the wasteland and swamp areas they had visited. There was no thought of Satan since she and Adam had nothing to do with him anymore after Father's warning.

"I wish Adam spent more time here at home with me." Whenever he returned from these forays, he shared his accomplishments with her, but he didn't have much to say about her preoccupation with the new room. It didn't occur to her that all she thought about was the room and caring for her baby with little else of interest.

Her creativeness soared uninhibited with decorating ideas while preparing the room. The angels had helped her cap the building on the outside with a tall steeple of topaz and bronze. The open arched windows lined its golden inner parlor. A high ceiling of azure with intricate jeweled designs topped the walls.

It was easy to make and kept her preoccupied when Adam was away. The materials to build the room, no matter how heavy, were lifted effortlessly or bent as she molded them with her thoughts and hands. [(1)] For her, there was no resistance, even with inanimate objects; everything complied to her will.

Uriel and other angels were always in attendance. They were as diverse in their personalities as any individual of the later human race, but were united in their servitude. Their varied abilities were at her disposal and they worked side by side with her, singing constantly. It made the work more enjoyable and she sang with them. Their songs blended in perfect harmony and there was never any silence. The theme was always about God.

Eve felt His presence continually surrounding them. He spoke to her throughout the day about His own ideas for children. *"I look forward to the day when your children are here! And their children! More and more to be with Me forever, for I am a God of abundance! I will help you teach them. They will have many talents and abilities. Each will be different and I have a plan for each of their lives."*

He projected His future plans for her children, but Eve was more concerned about her first baby. "I want it to be a surprise whether it's a boy or girl. So don't tell me! I know it will be a special child, the beginning of us as a family. I want to have family times together and children at my side as we care for Eden."

"Yes," He agreed. *"We'll have adventures together and cultivate the earth so more can live here and I can live with them. We'll be busy together! We'll reach great heights and have great victories! I will laugh with them and be so proud of them! What joyful times we will have!"* After a little pause, He added a bit more seriously, *"This is My perfect will."*

Eve enjoyed these times together, but one thing marred her happiness as she worked. Sometimes Adam would come home with Raphael and his thoughts were similar to those he had before when Father had corrected him. It was disquieting and she began to withdraw a little from him.

It was apparent he had difficulty getting these new ideas out of his mind and the cycle of doubting thoughts would reoccur, sometimes more frequently. Once he said to her, "There are other powerful beings in this world with free wills like ours. In their culture, it's wrong for a man-god to love another god. They think it wrong that I love Father." [2]

Uriel and Raphael gasped at this, but Adam seemed oblivious to their reactions. Eve shot back, "That is outlandish and shocking!" His words insulted her. Why would he say such things?

"Of course, I don't believe it." he responded. "But did you know Michael and the angels had a battle once a long time ago and they still want to fight? It was terrible, but we know peaceful co-existence is the way of God."

His ideas troubled her and she began to avoid him after that. "Father, please make Adam understand and make him spend more time with me," she prayed. When she questioned Him about Adam, the Spirit counseled her, *"Speak to your husband and he will listen, for you are one in the spirit and one in the Lord. Open your mouth and I will fill it with the right words, for he will listen. He recognizes wisdom when he hears it and he will respond to Me."*

"When should I do that, Father?" she asked. "Sometimes I don't like being with him when he talks that way."

"Do not avoid him, but speak the truth. Do not let the sun go down on your disgust. [3] *Don't delay. Reverence him and speak words of truth together with love. Be careful to listen only to My guidance and not your feelings. Truth will have its way and love never fails."* [4]

She was comforted then with the security of His support, but also sorry for avoiding Adam and found herself wanting to talk to him. Her devotion to him overrode her hurt and confusion at his remarks. She would do anything for him. Being one with him was all important now, especially with the expectation of their first child who was sure to arrive in the near future. Thinking of her baby caused her spirit to brighten again and she was excited to talk to Adam about it.

When he came home that day, she sat down with him, looked directly into his eyes, projected her thoughts to him, and the words naturally tumbled out. "I appreciate that you are tending Eden to make it a pleasant home for us. I love you and want to help too. I want to make this a wonderful place to have our family. How good it will be when we have our children here with us! We must continue to love God and teach our children to love and obey Him. We must not listen to anyone else who is not one with Father."

Adam listened and the Spirit opened his mind to the truth and he paused to consider it. Then, with remorse, he said, "I regret what I said and I apologize for disturbing you." Now that he was focused on her, he could feel her hurt. "I love you and will refrain from contemplating those thoughts again. I want to help you, too, with planning for our children." It was so gratifying to hear these words and Eve gushed with overwhelming love for him.

"I will work with you on the palace renovation instead of working in the wasteland areas," he promised. "We'll construct additional buildings, too, for our future children as they grow." They laughed together in anticipation. "I like creating something out of bare materials and especially while doing it together with you," he continued. "We will celebrate each time a new building is completed. Then I will play a psaltery and sing a ballad for you."

Eve glowed her approval. "And I will dance a pirouette!"

####

Adam was as good as his word. Days passed while he worked together with Eve on the palace room and the time slipped quietly by. But once they had renewed themselves to each other, they forgot to include God in their thoughts. They focused on the work and were also caught up in their mutual love, just as it was when they first came together, and for them, it was private.

Complacency for God had moved in and was not about to move out. For Eve, it was better to have time with her husband, though it was the Spirit that had counseled how to talk to him. For Adam, it was easier to be with Eve and ignore the newcomer than to expel him. That way, his conscience was eased and he didn't have to take a stand against Satan. After all, peace was God's way, wasn't it?

One day, God interrupted them. *"I want you to join Me more often each day. Set aside your building activities and be with Me."* So, they made a decision to spend the cool of the evenings each day with Him.

One such evening found them in the palace sitting quietly at His feet. Gabriel and Michael stood in attendance at either side of Him and Uriel and Raphael sat with Adam and Eve. Myriads of other angels encased the surrounding outer walls of the palace and sang quiet songs of respect and honor to God.

Waves of pure, white light radiated with brilliance out from Him and all around Him, but it was so soft that it didn't blind Adam and Eve, only saturated them completely with peace and holiness.

He began teaching them truths by relating to His creations beginning with the earth and leading up to their beginning, which He enjoyed speaking about, as any parent would.

They were entranced with irresistible reverence for Him, soaking in His overwhelming love. It permeated into every fiber of their being while He beamed with parental pride over them. His words seemed to penetrate down to their very bones, like streams of living water.

The importance of these revelations was almost lost on them, so enraptured they were with the story and His presence. Then He expounded on a particular person, His adversary.

"His name was Lucifer. I created him to be an archangel of the highest order ..."

XI. LUCIFER

God observed Adam and Eve carefully as He explained how Lucifer came to be. *"He was perfect in all his ways, full of wisdom and beauty. He stood shoulder to shoulder with Michael and Gabriel and in charge of the heavenly worship.*

"I clothed him in beautiful gems and endowed him with special musical ability. I gave him golden instruments to lead worship at My throne. He traveled to Eden often to bring light and worship of Me there also. [1]

"But he began to change and eventually he saw himself as irreplaceable. He thought himself comparable to Me in many ways. He gloried in his beauty and the respect and admiration that came from being close to Me." God scowled. *"Power appealed to him and he wanted to reign in the highest part of heaven and be reverenced more than Me.*

"The change in him was so very gradual. Pride took root in him and he wouldn't let it go. He wanted to exert his own will apart from Me. Once he declared he had such a right, he defiled his position by reserving a part of the worship for himself. Then he set up his own court of worshiping angels. It was the first and

worst sin ever. His intention was to usurp My authority and deceive the angels to regard him as a god higher than Myself. [2] *But he deceived himself more than anyone else."*

Father paused a moment, as if considering the facts before continuing. *"My holiness couldn't tolerate such an abomination and he knew it. I threw him out of My sight, making a humiliating show of him in front of his followers who hoped to reign with him. He became filled with violent anger and rebelled mightily. The iniquities of him and his followers were exposed to justify their expulsion. They were cast out of heaven, but they can never die because they are spirit beings who live continuously.* [3]

"He tried to rule the earth beyond the garden of Eden as his kingdom. He began to dominate and distort it. He couldn't create anything, only pervert what already existed. He manipulated huge animals, behemoths, to eat each other, which was never My will." [4]

Adam and Eve were aghast! They couldn't conceive of such a thing! How could one animal eat another? It seemed impossible, and yet God spoke of it as if it were only yesterday.

"He ranted and raged against Me, enticing chaos, and feeding off the glut of atrocities happening with his behemoths. He reigned with death because he knew how I loved life.

"He tried to take My place in the world, always perverting what was already created. Instead of love, there was cruelty; instead of gentleness, brutal aggression; instead of perfect health and vigor, deformities and sickness; for peace there was terror.

His followers are now dark demons and Lucifer calls himself Satan—the rebellious one—the "prince" of them and proud of it. He can disguise his true form by pretension, so beware!" [5]

God was silent for a moment as Adam and Eve realized for the first time that Satan was Lucifer and it startled them. He allowed them to ponder it before continuing. *"The earth reacted to their sin until his behemoths killed each other and their numbers diminished."*

Father's countenance seemed to shift at the thought of what happened after this. *"I created another place for him and all his evil angels, a fitting place, Sheol, where they will exist with all their wickedness. When their days of sin are fulfilled, their final punishment will happen. But their time of rebellion must run its course before their judgement is meted out and then they will be imprisoned there."* [6]

Father's tone lightened as He explained about His plan for the world. *"My Spirit only allowed the earth to be filled with life forms capable of reproducing their own kind, so there are no longer any giant meat-eating monsters. This was My will and I declared it to be good.* [7]

"The crown of this world is you. You are the masterpiece of all My creations. [8] *You are a better ruler, one more like Myself, who would not exploit My creatures, but cooperate with My Spirit to bring forth beauty and peace."*

His voice softened and He tenderly touched their shoulders. *"You have the privilege that Lucifer so desired but could never acquire—to be My children and be like Me. You have come straight from My heart and are My heart's desire—free spirits who choose to be with Me always. You are so bonded to Me that you are a part of Me and can't live without Me. I created you to be constantly drawn to Me so this world will never be without Me ... because we choose to be together."*

Adam and Eve looked at each other, then at Father with knowing smiles of gratitude. They knew how much He was an integral part of their lives. They couldn't live without Him.

"I have also created you to take Lucifer's place of worship at My throne, a very great privilege. The ability to sing and play musical instruments abides in you. My Spirit inspires you and that is why when you feel it, you will want to express it. This is a gift I have given no other creatures—only you and the angels."

Adam and Eve nodded and glowed with new understanding. They realized now why they felt so wonderfully uplifted when they sang to Him, especially when Adam played the psaltery, and why it felt so marvelously satisfying. *"I have also given you this gift to help you through difficult times. It will help you to focus on Me. Use it often."*

They thought on the concept of "difficult times" and what it could possibly mean, but Father continued. He swept His arm past the palace walls to encompass the surrounding landscape. *"My plan has always been for you and your children to expand your kingdom to include the entire world and to enjoy it along with Me. I want you to subdue it and grow it to its full potential. Surely all creation will bow to you and I can rightfully continue to bless you as well as protect all My beautiful creations."*

He leaned forward as He explained in earnest, *"The world is a physical one run by physical beings. In this way I can justifiably keep Satan out. He is a spirit and must have a physical personage to rule here, and he has none. Also, I have constrained Myself from ruling the world without you because I gave it to you. I gave you and your descendants the right to govern all the earth."* (9)

With all seriousness He added, *"I have given My word on this, which can never change. Only you can give permission who is to rule, for you are physical beings as well as spirit beings. Satan wants to enter you and rule through you, taking My place in your lives. He will deceive you to do this, so guard your hearts."*

His voice softened again as He revealed more. *"I also desire to rule through you and I will always ask clearly to dwell in your innermost part, in the heart of your being. I will never overstep what you won't freely give Me. I can direct your lives best if I have all your heart. You must trust that I will only love and care for you. I know the paths you will travel and can be there to guide you if you will let Me."* After a moment, He added solemnly, *"Then I can deal with Satan."*

He cautioned them, *"Be aware then, that Satan desires to gain authority on earth and must attempt to get it through you. He envies you. If you obey him, he will be this world's ruler and rightly so, because it would turn your kingdom over to him. He can try by deception, so beware! I can easily overpower him when you command him with My words and by My Spirit, so be careful and use them."*

He warned them again, *"The power to do this is with Me, but I can't legally move without your consent because I have given the world to you."* Adam and Eve silently meditated on "legalities". God's word was regarded as the law and anything that contradicted it must be illegal. Meekly, they heeded His advice.

"Once I have given My word that it is yours, I cannot take it back. I cannot contradict My word and take the world back. I am totally just. Can you see how much I trust you? You MUST abide by My words and trust Me in everything!"

For the first time, Adam and Eve realized their responsibility in the earth loomed larger than they ever thought possible. They had assumed God governed the world, with or without their consent.

"Satan is looking to regain control. He also covets revenge and will try to hurt Me through you. He is envious that you truly are My children and he is indeed My enemy. He would do anything to take My place as your father and control the world." (10)

These last words were spoken with such deadly seriousness that Adam and Eve reacted with startled bewilderment at the enormity of the situation. They had never faced an enemy before, and such a formidable adversary, one who attempted to thwart God Himself! After contemplating this for a bit, Adam asked, "Is there no way You can rightfully rule here without us?"

His question brought an easiness back to the conversation and a twinkle seemed to light up Father's eyes. He relished sharing wisdom with His son and explaining His secret plans. *"I never commit a promise without a condition. In this way, I have the right to interfere if the affairs on earth do not go well and My conditions aren't met. Lucifer lost his authority because he didn't reverence Me as God. I will always rule on earth where I am reverenced as Lord and God of all and give to those who trust Me."*

He fixed His gaze on both Adam and Eve, then gently added, *"But I will never take away your freedom to choose. It's the one quality that separates you from all other creatures. It puts you higher than the angels. It places you close to Me. It makes you compatible with Me, yet very dependent on Me. I want always to care for you.*

"You are in very truth My son and daughter and I am exceedingly pleased with you. You are in My heart and My thoughts and My eyes are constantly on you. But first, I must teach you about living with Me." This last statement was made with some reserve. They felt impressed that there was something beyond the life with Him that they knew now.

"There are conditions on your right to this life", He continued. *"Coping with physical needs and pleasures can complicate all endeavors. But it is easy when you are with Me. Listen to Me, yield constantly to My Spirit, and know that I can deliver you, no matter what happens."*

He had never spoken with such deep compassion or earnestness as now. His love was so tangible and lavish that it flowed out in rolling waves that flooded and saturated them. It took their breath away and made them feel weak and limp, and yet they basked in the magnificence of it. If they hadn't been in repose at His feet, they would surely have fainted.

"The conditions you know: a part of Eden belongs to Me, specifically the Tree of Knowledge of Good and Evil, and you aren't to eat of it. [11] *The tree isn't important. I could make many more like it, but your love for Me must be enough to heed My command. By reverencing what I say and not stealing what is Mine, you are honoring our relationship, and both of us will reign.*

"Beware of pride. It overtook Lucifer and is a possibility with anyone who has free choice." He paused again, as if to reinforce His words. *"In your fleshly desires, if you should make a mistake,*

I will be there to help and make it right again. But you must be honest with Me always, trust Me, and value our relationship enough to turn to Me if something goes wrong. My children, do you understand this?"

They nodded. His warning was repetitious and it felt unnecessary. They understood completely and their minds began to wander.

"There is so much more I want to tell you, but you can't understand it just yet. [12] *For now, just know that the day you turn away from Me and listen to anyone who takes My place, you shall surely die."*

Little did they know that day was at hand.

XII. The Tree

A gentle mist rose from the ground and softly framed the path ahead of Adam and Eve as they strolled through the heart of Eden. Their radiant light leaped ahead and blazed all around, completely illuminating the way. A soft breeze carried the lilting songs of angels in the distance.

"Do you think the baby will look like you or me?" Eve asked.

"I don't know," Adam replied. "I only know how great it will be to teach a little boy how to tend to Eden, or how to write God's words, or how to play the psaltery." It was a thrill to be talking about their first baby, almost as if the event were already here.

"I want to sing lullabies to our baby, like the songs the angels sing." Eve glowed with anticipation. "I want to show our son or daughter different plants and animals. Won't it be good when all our children sit round about Father? He will be our family patriarch and teach us wisdom and the secrets of life and goodness."

They ascended a foothill and creatures welcomed them everywhere, from tiny specks of life to immense creatures—buzzing, droning, chirping, or twittering their songs of exuberance. Even hills, fields, and rain in the distant mountains hummed their glad tidings. Branches on palm trees slapped together in synchronized motion when they drew near and their leaves clapped in unison with the wind trickling through them. [1] Bountiful flowers lifted their smiling faces and sang their quiet little ballads as they passed by.

Noise and motion and God were everywhere. His life was evident in each creation and His sustaining power was felt as they went along.

White clouds of angels filled the blue skies around them, flowing and ebbing like ocean waves. They were especially constant and vibrant with their cheerful songs to God. Their cherubic faces, gleaming and smiling, reflected their happiness while their wings fluttered in exhilaration like millions of butterflies. They were seraphs of servanthood and enjoyed every minute of it—intelligent celestials who served willingly with abundant joy.

All the world seemed to be singing an excited orchestra of happiness. Every creature they encountered seemed to burst with abundant vitality, as if tripping over themselves in a hurry to thrive, give birth, nurture their young, and thrive more. All displayed a united purpose to reproduce and sing to God without the necessity of destroying another creature. It was life as God intended and Adam and Eve walked along its vociferous path. [2]

They were aware of God enjoying all of this too, and smiling especially with pride on them. [3] "What a privilege Father has bestowed on us, that He chose us to begin a race of people!" Adam beamed. "It begins with our first baby!" Eve's enthusiasm had finally had an effect on him.

"More than that, we are special! He has chosen and set us apart from all these others to be his family. We can choose when and how to sing to Him or serve Him, not like the others. It's our choice!" Eve responded.

As they walked along, they talked only of the future and their family. They passed a herd of sheep and two skipping lambs accompanied them along the way. Their sweet faces with dainty pink noses and soft white fleeces offset their luminous dark eyes. They bucked and frolicked along the path, scampering back and forth. Baruch and Sky joined them as well and they all laughed at the lambs' antics.

The lambs expressed their own laughter with hilarious play—rearing, leaping, head butting, then racing each other. "You can't catch me!" "Yes I can!" They scuttled up the rock outcroppings along the way, then pretended to fall and strutted with unabashed glee.

Eventually the small party came to a serene mountain where God had taken Adam and Eve before. It was full of choice nard plants, fragrant cinnamon trees, fig trees, and pepper vines. The exuberance and salutations of the angels increased as they approached, announcing that this mountain in the center of Eden was God's holy mountain.

Adam and Eve meandered on, relishing the freshness of the day with the mountain fragrance beckoning them on. If they had been paying attention, they would have discerned the Spirit attempting to get their attention, but they were lost in their own private conversations centered on babies and future plans. Baruch and Sky strode with them while the lambs played along the way. The mist rose more prominently here.

They enjoyed an easy climb up the mountainside where trees were numerous until they reached a summit where two glorious trees stood apart from the others, beautiful and magnificent. One was the Tree of Knowledge of Good and Evil and they recognized it right away. It was a fir tree with leaves like the carob tree and it had immense height. Its bountiful pods were like the fruit of grapes with a fragrance that penetrated far down the mountain. [4] Its height reached well beyond the other trees and it emitted a bearing of stolid, silent indifference. Erect and proud, it stood apart from the others.

It seemed to ignore them as it stood silent and reserved with its ripe fruit dripping amidst its hanging boughs. It didn't sing its song to them, as all other creations did. It belonged to God and sang only to Him.

The other tree they also recognized as the Tree of Life and it also stood strong and tall, but its fruit was higher, more difficult to reach. Adam and Eve paid little attention to it since there had been so much concern about the other tree. They paused between the two trees in the cool of their shadows and continued their talk about their children, ignoring the trees.

The Spirit, however, was striving to extend an uneasy feeling on them. This was not the place to rest; temptation was too close. However, they couldn't be distracted and reclined for a welcomed rest. Baruch sprawled under the shade of another tree while Sky grazed nearby. The lambs jumped over some nearby bushes and scampered ahead in a mock race, scuttling away.

The Spirit hovered over them now with intensity, but Adam and Eve were oblivious, enjoying their respite beneath the shadows of the trees. What could possibly mar this beautiful day? Listening to the Spirit was not important just now.

There was a scratching sound behind them and they turned to see a huge serpent coiled and basking on a rock, blinking in the rays of their light. He resembled a dark green lizard more than a snake with stubby legs and sharp angled wings similar to bats wings. He smiled at them, "Good afternoon, my lords! It is good to see you!"

There was something different about this animal. Adam startled, then scrutinized the creature's eyes. "Do I know you?"

The serpent rose from its curled position to raise its head, stretching it to arch high and almost looked Adam straight in the eyes.

"Yes, indeed, my lord. We are friends. I am at your service. May I shake down some delicious fruit from yonder tree with its wonderfully ripe fruit for your pleasure? I can be up it in no time at all!"

The Spirit was falling more heavily on Adam and Eve by the second, sounding the alarm.

XIII. The Test

My son, if sinners entice you, do not consent.
Proverbs 24: 10. New King James
None of the devoted things shall cleave to
your hand; that the Lord may turn from the
fierceness of His anger and show you mercy,
and have compassion on you, and multiply
you, just as He swore ... if you obey the voice
of the Lord your God, keeping all His com-
mandments ... and doing what is right in the
sight of the Lord your God.
Deuteronomy 13:17, 18. Revised Standard

Instantly Adam discerned who this was. The clever words were familiar and he recognized his former acquaintance. Satan had apparently expanded his territory beyond the swamp and outskirt wilderness areas because Adam didn't come there anymore. He had invaded further into Eden and transformed himself into the body of a serpent. [1]

But Adam was not the same; the gullibility was gone and he had more wisdom now. The caution he had learned from God slowly took over and he reminded himself that he had decided not to listen to Satan ever again.

But before he could turn away, Eve responded, "We can't eat from this tree."

Quickly the serpent replied. "Is that so? Hasn't God said you can have fruit from every tree in the garden?"

Eve smiled. "Of course, we can eat fruit from the trees in Eden! But the fruit of this tree God has said we must not eat, or even touch it, or we will die."

The serpent smiled back. "Surely you won't die! God knows that when you eat this fruit, the eyes of your souls will be opened to know everything about good and evil and you will be wise, like God is. Else why would this be the Tree of Knowledge of Good and Evil? [2] Hasn't God created everything to be good? And has He really said you can't touch it?"

Neither Adam nor Eve perceived this conversation was different than conversations they had with other animals or the angels. The serpent spoke with confusing variables: they wouldn't die if they ate the fruit, they would be wise like God was, everything God created was good, and did God say they couldn't touch the fruit?

The serpent also spoke from a viewpoint comparable to theirs—having the same position of authority. But he did seem to have a connection with them similar to the animals, and Eve especially was caught off guard. She conversed with the serpent as she always did with animals. The conversation happened quickly and the content seemed unimportant to her. It wasn't unusual, and now that the subject was fruit, she became hungry for it and had a sudden interest in it.

She and Adam didn't realize that their concentration on their future children during the day had distracted them and dulled their senses to anything the Spirit might have been saying at this crucial moment or to the danger at hand. They didn't sense His alarm.

The discussion with the serpent seemed to blend with their relaxed stroll through Eden and they weren't aware that the focus on their aspirations was taking precedence over everything else. As at a previous time, they had disconnected from God and were not listening to Him. They needed a quick readjustment to discern something adverse was presenting itself, but they weren't paying attention. In earnest, the Spirit grappled for their attention, but it was useless.

In that instant, all eternity seemed to hold its breath, but they were unaware of it. The destiny of all mankind was at a crossroads and held in the balance. The fate of all would be determined forever by what they did.

To Eve, this was just a snippet conversation with a serpent during their walk. The fruit looked good to her. Maybe it could make one wise; could that be wrong? What could it hurt to just touch it? She didn't remember God saying not to touch it.

She didn't realize that these thoughts that floated into her mind weren't her own. The fruited pod was within arm's length, dripping with juice. It couldn't hurt to touch it and impulsively she stood and plucked it, bringing it to her nose and smelling it. It couldn't be wrong just to smell it. Did God say she couldn't smell it? It smelled sweet and wonderfully delicious. It was so natural to eat fruit in Eden and without hesitation or thinking, she took a bite.

Adam stood up in shock beside her. It all happened so quickly he could hardly believe it. He could have interrupted her, but he was slow to respond. He hesitated to confront Satan, whom he had previously chosen to ignore instead of making the uncomfortable decision to expel him from Eden. Satan had been no threat to him, and now it was easier to stand by in numb silence.

So, the great moment had come, and sin reared its ugly face. It wasn't the face of Satan or temptation, but the silence of inaction and complacency. Adam's reaction was to become the foundation for the enemy of life—hesitation, apathy, and rethinking something instead of taking a bold action to protect and guard.

Immediately after the first bite, Eve was aware without a doubt that what she had done was wrong. She could rationalize it away—she was hungry and the fruit looked delicious. But a horrible feeling of guilt slowly replaced the hunger in the pit of her stomach. She had stolen what belonged to God and suddenly she felt all alone. It was something she had never felt before and as it began to combine with her guilt, it produced a fear that mounted in strength by the second and left her floundering in distress.

As the horror of it began to slowly overwhelm her, she turned to Adam and their eyes locked. They didn't need to talk about what just happened. They knew they were separated—one was guilty, one was not. It wasn't hunger Adam felt in his stomach like Eve did. It was alarm, and for the first time, grief, though he didn't know what grief was or how to compare it to anything he had ever felt before. It was a sickening feeling that started small but grew quickly in intensity. It was too uncomfortable to bear. He didn't want to address it, only be rid of it as quickly as possible.

Eve extended her hand to him with the fruit in it, inviting him to join her. She had to share her distress with him! She couldn't handle this alone!

He understood completely what it would mean if he refused to eat the fruit. If he didn't stand with Eve and share her guilt. He would be totally separated from her. To be without her was unthinkable, but the thought of living without God never entered his mind. He didn't want to ask the Spirit what to do—He might tell him to leave Eve and it was impossible to conceive of life without her. He knew well enough what it was like to be alone. He and Eve must be one and live together forever. That was the plan.

"I could never go back to living like that again—to be alone," he thought. He rebelled against the thought of forsaking her and refused to consider it. But could he actually turn against God?

These thoughts passed quickly through his mind in one moment and he withdrew from considering any repercussions. He couldn't process any thought that God could create another woman for him just as easily as He had made Eve. It would never be the same. He was devoted to her alone.

At the same time, he felt a strong, unusual pressure to make the decision now, but it was too quick, too sudden to ponder. He gasped at the reality of what just happened and how to respond.

Eve felt him waver and received a sudden thought to impress him to hurry and join her. She didn't consider where the new thought came from, but she couldn't bear holding this horrible feeling by herself. Her mind was screaming, "I need his comfort and help!" She reached out and put the fruit in his hand.

In the end, the caution God had given about consulting Him for help—listening to the Spirit and using His commanding words to overcome a problem—was not a consideration in Adam's mind.

The mist that had accompanied them throughout the day slowly rose from the ground and turned darker at each passing moment. It swirled and started to billow up around them as Adam took and ate the fruit. (3)

XIV. The Curse

Adam and Eve stared at each other as the gloom in the pit of their hearts spread and enveloped their entire bodies. At first, they stood there, stunned. Their initial thought was to flee, but they found they were no longer able to lift into the air. Their spirits that had soared with easy freedom were now being dragged down with their bodies in a way they had never felt before. It was the heavy pressure of gravity that pulled on their bodies and inhibited their flight. It crushed them, making it difficult to breathe, and pressed them to the ground.

Their light was quickly fading also with only the stark outline of their physical bodies remaining, plain and fleshy.

The serpent changed too. He quickly transformed into a harassing creature who writhed in delight. His smile morphed into a hateful grimace. "Look at you! You're naked! How shameful! Your bodies are ugly and everyone can see your nudity! What will God think of you?" For the first time in their lives, they realized the vulnerability of their exposed naked bodies and blushed, turning away.

Appalled and embarrassed, they sent commands to the surrounding flora. "Quick! Cover us!" But their thoughts came back with no response. Alarmed, they crouched like animals in wonderment at what exactly was happening. Fumbling and stumbling among the trees and brush, they groped for something—anything—that could cover them or be a way of escape. If only they could rise up to the sky and get away as they had always done before!

They had lost their glory and began to know terror for the first time while the serpent taunted them loudly so every spirit within earshot was sure to hear. "You have obeyed me! That makes me the new ruler! I am lord once again! I have taken Eden from God's stinking brats! And that's not all! The entire world belongs to me now!"

Something else had changed. Besides the gloating serpent and themselves, all was quiet. They had always taken for granted the constant angelic music, but now they realized it was much too quiet. Desperately they searched for angels, but none were in sight. The angels had to be there, but there was no response to their pleas for help. How was this possible?!

Baruch and Sky stood by and they sent their thoughts to them next. "Baruch! Sky! Please come!" Surely the strength of the lion and a swift ride on the mare would escort them away! But Baruch only prowled around them, indecisive and confused. For the first time he couldn't hear their thoughts and they couldn't hear his. He growled at them instead with a fear he had never shown before. He veered away from the serpent and crept into the bushes like Adam and Eve. Remarkable! Huge and powerful Baruch was afraid of a serpent!

Sky skittered nervously just out of range as she also sensed terror for the first time and she didn't respond to Eve's call. She stared blankly at Eve, expecting a word from her, but she didn't receive any of Eve's thoughts. The typical pathway of instant communication between them was broken.

With the connection to Adam and Eve completely gone, the lion and mare retreated into the rising fog with perplexity, unable to comprehend the need for their help. Adam and Eve screamed at them in desperation, for surely these steadfast companions would never leave them! But the two animals only melted away faster into the gathering shadows in fear. It was impossible to believe!

It was then that Adam and Eve began to realize they had lost their spiritual sight and hearing. They crouched in bewilderment and confusion. How could things be so pleasant and carefree one moment, and the next, after the simple act of plucking and eating fruit, their light was gone, their flight was gone, and all the world had been transformed? Spiritual darkness seemed to close in around them along with the mist.

Eve felt the turmoil of panic building stronger with each passing moment and she sobbed uncontrollably. Then she realized her sorrow wasn't heard by anyone; her thoughts were returning to her unacknowledged. "What are we going to do?! What are we going to do?!" Her words were garbled from her mouth, not her thoughts. Something warm and wet was rolling out of her eyes and down her cheeks.

Adam hugged her, then timidly pulled away. As her light receded, revealing the blank, open exposure of her body, he couldn't help staring at her naked form. The frank reality of her nudity caused a surprising and concupiscent sensation in him, despite the enormity of the situation.

At the same time, he disregarded the embarrassment he was causing her. He saw only her body, not the companion he loved. Without the guidance and good sense of his spirit, the selfish lust of his own body overwhelmed him, even at this inappropriate time. It was the preamble to all the human race—coping with strong physical senses without the wisdom of a living spirit. His pure and wholesome spirit was dying and his soul began to struggle. He gulped and turned from her, conscious of his own nakedness.

The two clung to the bushes, frightened and completely at a loss as what to do. The mist swirled up from the ground and became a dank fog, dripping on their skin. Desperate and shivering, they tore fig leaves from stalks and frantically tied them together with vines around their waists to hide their nudity. [1] The thin leaves made miserable coverings and they felt miserable in them.

The serpent laughed at their feeble attempts, gloating in his moment of triumph. "You belong to me now and you will be my slaves forever! Everything will be under my control and your cursed God can't stop it because He's so damned "just" all the time! He can't break His own word, so He can't take you back because now you're like me—sinners! I outsmarted Him once and for all!"

His words stung deep into their souls like flaming darts, festering the guilt they were struggling to control. But nothing stopped his tyrannical accusations. "You fools! Spoiled brats you are! Oh, it was all so easy! I can hardly wait to see the look on His face when He sees you sniveling on the ground!"

Adam and Eve covered their ears to stop his insane barrage. The thought of Father seeing them like this was more than they could bare. They shrieked in fear and covered their faces with trembling hands.

Satan uncoiled the length of his body to boldly rear his head and stare close up at Adam, face to face. "I will toy with you until you have your 'precious' children. I will overwhelm them like I have done with you and they will follow me before I kill you all off! They will be my children now, not God's! [2] You'll bow before me! I'll decide about everything you do!" He spat on the half-eaten fruit lying on the ground and it began to turn a rusty brown.

They did bow before him, after a fashion. They groveled in the dirt, sinking in despair while he hurled insulting threats that caused them to sob in anguish. What had they done to deserve this? Why couldn't they flee?

He bombarded them with waves of fear. "From now on you will be afraid of going hungry and being homeless. You will know want, failure, loneliness, rejection, brokenness, sickness, and most of all, death, where I will ultimately rule!"

Aghast, Adam and Eve quivered in a cold sweat and clung to the trees and underbrush like hunted animals. Reeling with desperation and confusion, they cried out for help.

But there was no help and it had no effect on the serpent. He relished their misery. "Your fear and foolish attempt to hide your mistake will be inherited by all your children. They will inherit it from you! You won't even be able to protect them! You are guilty of passing your own violation on to your children and they will do the same as you, trying to hide their mistakes!"

Adam and Eve wailed in despair and regret, but it didn't make any difference. Satan continued, "I will be their father and rule their hearts and souls! They will be like me instead of you! They will be full of lust, selfishness, violence, hate, and will turn against your God, just like me! They will know only fear their entire lives! The days of freedom are over for all of you! I've planned this for a long time and now it's happening!"

With vehemence he spat out the threats. "I will draw your children away from God. They will become addicts and be drained of life. It will crush your hearts and there will be no relief! I will drive every husband and wife apart. They will be unfaithful and sick in their minds and depressed. They will loathe each other and abandon their stupid commitments. I will draw them after other lovers and it will never end! They will be greedy for riches. They will murder for it!"

His gleeful rants continued. "Anger will be out of control because they will taste my anger for your ridiculous God. They won't be able to stop their violence and will love it like I do. Not only that, but all those dumb creatures that He thought were so great are going to be under my control, and your failure will spread to them too, as well as everything else. I'll put sickness on everything He created and make them suffer long and hard. I will love it! I'll kill, steal, and destroy! [3] Everyone's going to suffer!"

His antagonisms dominated the heavy silence hanging in the air that now surrounded them. Adam and Eve sobbed in submission while dark and gloomy clouds overhead heralded the approach of a storm.

And that is how God found His children.

XV. In the Throne Room

And the Lord was sorry He had made man
on the face of the earth, and He was grieved
in His heart. Genesis 6:6. New King James

Therefore I said, look away from Me. I will
weep bitterly. Do not labor to comfort Me
because of the plundering ... of My people.
For it is a day of trouble and treading down
and perplexity ...
> Isaiah 22:4-5. New King James

God called for Adam and Eve, but He didn't approach them
immediately. His voice rang out from His throne room and
rolled down the mountain where they were cringing and
wailing.

Higher on the mountain, a golden ladder with intricate
railings could be seen through the mist leading up to His
throne room. It spanned millions of miles into the sky and

the royal loftiness of it increased as it ascended in height. At the bottom was a gate whose posts shook with what sounded like a thousand crashing waters. [1]

It was God's voice and the area was filled with His sorrowful lament. Smoke furled in the blurry vapors along the ladder as He called out, *"Where are you, Adam? My son, where are you? Where are you, Eve, My daughter? Come to Me! I'm waiting for you!"* It was the heart cry of a father who had lost His children.

Along the ladder were a multitude of angels of every size and description. [2] They darted about the rungs leading up to Him, shouting alarm now rather than singing. God was seated at the top in His throne room with His sparkling robe billowing out and filling the surrounding expanse. Lightning bolts flashed about Him with crashing thunder and the foundation of the throne room quaked. Brilliant, fiery rays shot out from Him and illuminated the entire area while fire and lightning blazed about the throne.

At the foot of the throne Michael and Gabriel bowed low before God. Their huge bulk was dwarfed by the magnificence and intensity of the Lord. But their shoulders slumped in shame, as if they had been the ones caught in disobedience, and they couldn't face God in His grief. They bent in reverent veneration, their faces on the floor and their wings outstretched and flat, pointing toward Him in somber ambiance.

Above His throne was an array of mighty angels, each with a set of three fiery wings. With the top pair they covered their faces in disgrace: they were horrified to see God's children sinning. With the middle pair they excitedly fluttered about the throne. With the bottom pair they covered their feet as a sign of humbleness before Almighty God. While they flew about the throne, they shouted excitedly as if nothing had changed, "Holy! Holy! Holy is the Lord of all creation!" [3]

Myriads of other angels also flew around the throne, but in more quiet worship with somber attentiveness. They were embarrassed for the event they had just witnessed and uneasy with the hurt they knew God felt, yet their worship to Him never ceased.

He seemed not to notice their activity, but was intent on what was transpiring in Eden. He was not caught off guard with the success of Satan's temptation. He had always known what would happen to Adam and Eve, but His wrath was furious, nonetheless. Jealousy of Satan taking His place in the hearts of His children burned hot and He was infuriated with losing them to Satan's tactics.

"That liar! That thief! That sly deceiver! [4] *Behold, I will cast him and his demons out forever and heal My children! He hasn't won! When the time is perfect, I will accomplish it!"* He clenched His fists in anger and the angels recoiled. Thundering clouds brooded and swirled about Him and lightning flashed from the clouds.

The angels responded by picking up the urgency for what looked like certain war and raised their hands in allegiance, now shouting a battle cry. "The Lord is mighty and powerful! Who can stand before Him?!" They were glad for an opportunity to do something. To see their God this furious was foreign to them and they awaited a command.

But His rage eventually abated and He sat in silence for a long time. Even the storm around Him subsided. He ignored the angels, then heaved a deep sigh and groaned. *"Oh, how I want to hold My children and protect them, like a hen gathers her chicks beneath her wings! But they believed Satan and fell into his trap. Now they are desolate!* [5] *Why didn't they listen to Me? I could help them still if they would only turn to Me, as I promised! But they won't! My grief is beyond deepest understanding. My heart is crushed! Listen to the weeping of My people across the land!"*

He was viewing generations of people down through the centuries as they followed Adam's lead. He knew each person already, before they were even born. They were as real and alive to Him as Adam and Eve and just as much His children. But now, every one of them would live with desperation and suffering. There would be oppression, abuse, torture, and worse. Coping with Satan without God's Spirit would be too horrendous for any of them to endure. They would feel the sting of death and the consequences of separation from Him. How could He forsake them?

"They will ask, 'Where is the Lord? Has He deserted us?' For the hurt of My people, I am hurt. I am mourning." [(6)]

Then His thoughts returned to Adam and Eve.

"My children! Oh, My children! It is not so much that they stole from Me, but that they will turn to each other now and not to Me! They won't remember My words to trust and reverence Me, but will trust each other and follow Satan instead! They have chosen to abide by Satan's words and his fear will fill their hearts. They will only hear him now and not My Spirit. They don't know what that will cause them! They will never survive without Me! I have made them to be incomplete without Me. They don't know how malicious Satan is! They don't know the heartache ahead of them! Now more than ever they need Me! How I long to rescue them!"

He lamented at length in utter hurt for them, but it was apparent to the angels His grieving words weren't meant for Himself only. He was talking to someone else.

"Their spirits are dying already!", He addressed that other person. *"Their souls and bodies will struggle to regain the spiritual life they had in Me until it ends in a final death when Satan snatches them away. [(7)] He will turn life into death now and will use it to its fullest extent. He will control it. [(8)] When he causes their bodies to die, their souls will fall into the final abode I made for him and his demons, but it was never meant for My people!*

How can I let that happen?! How can I forsake them? If only they would turn to Me!!" Slowly, He added, *"But I can't force them."*

He stood before His throne then with a quiet reserve. Crashing thunder sounded again around Him and the clouds ignited with flashes of violent light in response. It intensified in magnitude and a sound like the roar of a huge crowd or like the smashing waves of hundreds of ocean tsunamis striking shorelines filled the throne room. It grew louder with each passing moment until it reached a crescendo of turbulent strength and power. [9].

It swirled around His throne, engulfing it until it became a huge mass of fierce, radiating energy. It engulfed Him completely and transformed Him into an unrecognizable ball of fire. Tiny particles of moving, silver-like crystals darted around within the nimbus as it swelled and churned, then rotated in throbbing revolutions.

It pulsated like this for some time until it seemed it would burst. Then a figure breached out from the midst of it. It resembled a man and He stepped out from the center of the vibrating mass. [10]

He looked similar to the angels except He had no wings. He wore a startlingly white robe with a gold band around His chest and His hair shone white from radiance beaming out of Him. [11] He turned and faced the tremendous ball of light until it subsided and the Father's form could be seen again.

For a long while they faced and regarded each other until the Godly figure responded to the Father's remarks. They conversed for some time and it was evident the God-Man knew the Father intimately. Both shared the agonizing thoughts of Adam and Eve's dilemma and the loss of their kingdom to Satan.

"Adam and Eve's submission to Satan will cause a seed of rebellion and corruption that will be planted firmly in their souls,

even at this moment," the God-Man said, *"and it will not stop with them. It will spread to their children."* (12)

"*It is compounded by their disregard for Me,"* Father added in repugnance. *"But most of all it will grow into a worsening condition. Unless they turn again to Me, they will pass that rebellion on to their descendants and death will replace My plan for life on earth."* (13)

Father's disgust about the situation caused His fury to rise again and the angels heard Him say to the God-Man angrily, *"Let them follow each other and Satan then, if that's what they want! I relinquish all ties to them! Now go! Leave Me alone that My just wrath may burn hot. I will start all over again, and make a great nation from You!"* (14)

XVI. JUSTICE

The God-Man pleaded with the Father. *"Why have You given up on Our children? Won't Satan say We have created them and yet We couldn't save them from his hand? Turn from Your fierce wrath and relent from this.* [1] *Remember You swore to bless them with many children. You wanted a family from them, and behold, Our plan has never changed! From the beginning of time We knew this would happen."*

Father listened and relented, for the God-Man knew the Father's heart, but He was saddened and grieved beyond comprehension. What hurt the worse was that Adam and Eve knew the love He had for them, but they wouldn't depend on that love and ask forgiveness or turn to Him to deliver them from their crisis.

"How I long for them to seek Me for help!" Father lamented. *"But they are attempting to deal with the situation themselves. As innocent as it looks to them, it reveals their belief they can cover their disobedience without coming to Me with a contrite heart and ask forgiveness."*

The God-Man replied, *"We can't forgive them without repentance, because then they would never completely return to*

You. It would prevent them from being wholeheartedly compatible with You. They have opened themselves to Satan's wiles by accepting his attitude into themselves, and it will penetrate down to the very heart of their character and soul."

Father groaned. *"If they continue in it, they must have the same punishment that was meant for evil. That mistrust and attitude would become so much a part of them that it will pass down to future generations. And their compromise with Satan would not happen just once. It would affect every part of their lives in the future. Adam would expect his own independent thoughts and lifestyle could be combined with Our plan for him without any repercussions."*

The immediate circumstances were hiding it, but God saw this in the future. He knew Adam and Eve would blatantly continue in their subtle rebellion against Him, no matter how innocent the situation looked to them.

He observed the couple on earth and their groveling among the trees. Their fear of Him was mounting by the minute under Satan's cruel accusations, shaming them into disloyalty to Him.

"There is also another consideration," Father added. *"It can't deny My justice. It is Who I Am. To have no consequence for Adam and Eve's acceptance of Satan's words and admitting him into their lives is not an option. It's an affront I can't overlook as a just God. I am intolerant of all evil.*

"They have disregarded My one command—a command meant for good to restrain them from evil. Now it interferes with My compassion for them, but there must be justice! It is impossible for Me to do otherwise. I can never change." (2)

He stopped for a moment before continuing. *"I also can't go against My word once it has been given and remove the binding agreement I have with them. I proclaimed a true and uncompromising promise that they would rule the earth starting with Eden and I can't take it back. My word is a holy vow and I can't go against it - even now after they have abandoned Me and turned their kingdom over to Satan - and Satan will never give it back."* [3]

Together Father and the God-Man reviewed the situation. They knew the downward spiral of the world would never end unless something were done to interrupt and divert it. Father spoke with resolve, *"People must first seek My will, then I will take fire from My Spirit and purge corruption out of them.* [4] *If they do that, I will restore the authority I gave to Adam. I can't force them, for I made mankind to always have a free will."*

After a long pause, He spoke more softly. *"But they won't understand. They won't be able to see or hear Me and our enemy will deceive them.* [5] *My Spirit can talk to them and some will listen, but others won't comprehend. My people need to hear My words spoken plainly so they understand, but they will be intrigued with the excitement of listening to another spiritual leader, just like their father Adam".*

He gazed at the God-Man a long time before adding, *"But We have planned what We would do long ago about how We will deliver them. We can win them back. This curse can be reversed."*

As the two faced each other, their eyes locked and their thoughts intertwined like a one-sided conversation. They knew what it would take to explain Their plan of deliverance to people and who would reveal it to them.

Father spoke quietly, *"An angel can't do it. Only another man can take back the world from Satan, one who doesn't follow Adam's affiliation to him. I can't participate in the lives of people anymore unless another man, a holy man with a heart to continually obey and honor Me, goes to them and explains Our plan for them to be delivered from Satan and suffering."*

The God-Man nodded in agreement. *"I feel Your love for these people. We both know that the person You speak of must be a man who knows You intimately and can reveal You accurately to the masses of peoples. He must win their hearts and souls so they believe him without seeing You. He has to show them how much We love them and they must trust him to the very end. Then he can bring them back to You."*

He stopped then because He knew the plan He and Father had meted out long ago and what it would entail. His heart was stirred with the challenge.

Father continued, *"Otherwise, I can only standby and watch as mankind deteriorates because I made the world a physical one, ruled only by mankind. I created it so it could only be ruled by a good person, a man after My own heart, not ruled by spirits like Satan. But this physical world ruled by men also alienates Me."*

The God-Man finished the thought, *"Only a righteous man who is just like You can save the world."*

Father resumed, *"He would have to stand between the people and Me, to divert the punishment and receive what they deserve, because I am a righteous God. Evil has to be sentenced and punished, for We can't let it prevail. After Our children are protected and set aside from Satan, then he will pay his just dues."*

As He spoke the words, Father knew. They both knew what this would entail. *"That man must replace Adam as My son,"* Father spoke softly. *"He has to be as innocent as Adam was at the beginning. He also has to be My son because all other peoples will inherit Adam's seed of rebellion and servitude to Satan. He has to be perfect before me, for I am a righteous God. Yet he must speak to people in a way they can understand so they will accept him as My son and know he represents Me. Then he has to remove their sin to open a way back to Me. They must be as holy and pure of heart as You are."*

Just as the God-Man knew Father God's heart, so Father knew the Godly-Man's heart. Father was filled with wrenching grief. He knew the words would penetrate the heart of the God-Man and move Him with the same compassion He had for people. It was a compassion that was so deep and full it reached down to the very depth of His being.

But the choice had already been made long ago and it hadn't been a little decision. They had made the decision to

101

create the human race because of the love They had for children. That love was worth the sacrifice they knew must now happen.

This Son of God had to step down from all the glory of heaven and accept the consequences of Adam and Eve's failure as well as that of all mankind. The sacrifice would be horrific, but justice demanded a penalty.

Father God spoke softly, knowing the immensity of that sacrifice. It would have a lasting effect, not only between the two of Them, but upon everyone on earth. *"The only way this can be accomplished is for My son to be born a man the same as everyone else so he can represent all people as a son of the human race, and then take their punishment in one moment of time. That punishment has to be equal to the crimes of all humanity for it to satisfy the requirement of justice, and it will mean suffering of the worst kind. People won't take punishment like that and I won't put them through it."*

Father scrutinized the God-Man's face with deep grief. Though the decision had been made eons ago, He was presenting it to the God-Man again. It wasn't too late to back out. *"It will be the ultimate sacrifice, not only for My son, but for Me. I will know of his suffering—it will crush My heart—and I also risk losing him to eternity if he should join mankind in their determination to stray from Me. But if he chooses to offer his life for theirs, it will cover and protect My children from that punishment throughout every generation."*

His concern and sympathy for every person born in the future rolled out like a flood and drenched the God-Man, yet justice had to prevail. *"There has to be punishment for crimes: evil has to be judged and punished. I can't allow evil to prevail. It has to be addressed or all is lost! A substitute person taking that punishment is the only answer. Then My people can come to Me again. I will put in their hearts a longing to know Me and they will respond if they can understand how much I love them. When I give everything I have for them, even My one and only son, they will come back to Me!*

"When that punishment is done, and the people accept My son, His holiness will cover them and it will take away their rebellion. They will be set free from death and live forever with Me. My will is that people live with Me and that they live in abundance. [6] *Yet they must retain their free will and receive it."*

The God-Man knew already about the abhorrent punishment for the entire world's sins. This son of God would have to become a man with a physical body and feel suffering like any other human, and they both knew the final punishment Father spoke about would be horrific. But unless this happened, every person would be lost forever because they would be born under Satan's rule that was now being quickly established on earth and they would succumb to his devices. They would be deceived and think they were right with God, only to find they had aligned themselves with His enemy. Being drawn away to evil was so wrong!

Father God's heart surged with anguish when He thought of it. He had to save His children no matter the cost! How could He let them be with Satan in everlasting punishment? Never! *"I must send someone to save them! I must deliver them out of Satan's hand."*

There was only one who could do this, who had the pure nature of God and could withstand the task. He had to reverence Father and keep the agreement, not like Adam had done. He had to understand that it was a sacred agreement, and not break it.

The God-Man bowed His head in reverent obedience and presented His appeal, recommitting Himself, just as He had done long ago, *"Here I am. Send Me. Make Me Your son!"* [7]

There was relief then, but also much sorrow as the Father embraced the God-Man with many tears. The God-Man fell on Father's neck and wept a good long time, yet their love for people overrode their sorrow. [8] They both knew it was an immense task followed by an excruciating death to provide a sacrifice capable of removing all the world's sins. But the effort was worth saving the lives of multitudes of people, of whom They both foresaw, and They already felt overwhelming compassion for them.

Father placed His hand on the chest of the God-Man, groaned, and solemnly proclaimed, *"This day I beget Thee and this day I proclaim Thee as My Son. I also commit You as a son to mankind. You will be My son as well as their son. When You petition Me on behalf of Your people, I will forgive them because You have paid for their crimes. They will turn to You for deliverance and You shall break Satan's rule over them with an iron rod and scatter all rebellion. Then You will inherit all the kingdoms of the world, even unto the ends of the earth, as Your possession.* (9) *For You will conquer death once and for all! You shall be King of Kings and Lord of Lords, because You are willing to lay down Your life for My people. Great will be Your reward!"*

But it wasn't the reward of many kingdoms that moved the God-Man—now the Son of God. It was compassion for the myriads of suffering people yet to be born and the desire to relieve them that He felt the most.

Father continued, *"Behold, I also commit all judgement to You, that all should honor You just as they honor Me. He who does not honor You does not honor Me. Assuredly everyone who hears Your words and believes Me—that I sent You—will have a full life with Me in eternity and shall not come under judgement, even if they are not perfect, because they pass from death to life.* (10)

"It is such a simple plan; how can people resist? All they need is to accept My son on their behalf—just take into their hearts the mercy I extend to them through My son—and follow Our Spirit. I will make it plain with written words I will give them for safekeeping unto all generations. Even their youngest will understand it.

"They will still have free choice, but for those who choose You, their spirits will be revived and they will hear Me again. I will make it so easy for them!"

Father thought of His son and the world's future. *"Oh, My son! Fail Me not, for all the world is at stake! And yet My heart is heavy! How can I give You up and hand You over to My enemy? You will see utter destruction at his hand! How can I put all that on You? My heart churns within Me! My sympathy is overwhelming!"* [11]

Then, one more declaration: *"You are My precious son, and whoever understands this and refuses to accept Your sacrifice—Our sacrifice—will have to answer to Me. And there will be no other sacrifice that can cover them."*

They left the throne room together, embracing with determination and resolve in their voices. [12] In privacy, they expounded on their dedicated promises: when the time was right, the son would live on earth as any other man, teach people about the Father's love, rescue them from Satan's clutches, and restore them to God.

The son reassured His father that He would carry His love for people always in His heart and the Father reassured His son that He would validate Him as His son while He was on earth. [13] This was to prove he was sent from God, and was God's own son. Father would always be with Him, except when the son underwent the condemnation of the world and take its punishment in one final sacrifice. Then Father would remove His protection and allow the sentence to be enacted.

Father spoke a word of comfort. *"I will show You what to do with My Spirit and always be with You."* They sat and partook of a heavenly meal, sealing their promises. Then they discussed their plan and how they would present it to Adam and Eve.

XVII. Consequences

The joy of our heart is ceased; Our dance has
turned into mourning.
The crown has fallen from our head. Woe to us,
for we have sinned!
Because of this our heart is faint. Because of
these things ... our eyes grow dim ...
Renew our days as of old. Unless You have
utterly rejected us,
And are very angry with us!

Lamentations 5:15-17, 21, 22. New King James

God approached Adam and Eve from a distance without the
regular foray of angels and pomp, but He didn't come directly to
them. He called to them up and down the expanse of Eden for
hours while the fog turned cold and the clouds grew heavier with
darkness. He waited, giving them every opportunity to come
to Him for help. But for the first time, Adam and Eve wished

He would go away as fear of Him gripped their hearts. Running away was a stumbling impossibility, as much as they wanted to, because fear was progressively overwhelming and immobilizing them. They only managed to crouch among the trees. [1]

The light around God glared stronger as He drew near, pushing aside the darkness. It was blinding and obliterated everything in sight, and yet He continued to call. The ground heaved and trembled at His approach while the fog swirled on the fringes just beyond His light. They cringed low on the ground and covered their eyes against the severity of His holiness, cowering and whimpering at the exposure of their shame. If only they could hide from Him!

Suddenly He was there, surveying the scene. For some strange reason, His face looked more like the angel they had previously walked with, but they were so miserable they hardly noticed. His demeanor and regal majesty were characteristic of the God they always knew.

He ignored the serpent, who at last was silent, and after a long pause He spoke to Adam, addressing the state Adam found himself in. *"Where are you now?"* [2]

Adam groveled on the ground in perfect misery, "I heard Your voice in the garden and didn't want You to see me naked. So, I hid." It didn't occur to him that God already knew what had happened or why He asked the question.

But God had a reason for asking. He had to give Adam a chance and prodded him for an honest confession. *"Who told you that you were naked? Have you eaten fruit from the Tree of Knowledge of Good and Evil that I commanded you not to eat?"* [3]

Adam groveled as he struggled to project the words through the fear in his mind and squirmed, "The woman whom You gave to be with me took the fruit and gave it to me and ..." (after a long pause), "I ate it."

Somehow it was better if the blame was first spread to Eve before admitting his own guilt. [4] He was telling the truth after all, or so he thought. God did give him Eve (now reduced in status to "the woman"), and she did give him the fruit. But he was throwing the blame first in a different direction before admitting his own error and shouldering the full responsibility alone. At the same time, by subtly blaming God for giving him Eve, he was involving God in the deed. But it put God on the same plane as himself, a terrible mistake!

Eve was taken aback at his answer. It was a total relinquishing of his devotion both to her and God to save himself. She never would have believed Adam would do such a thing if she hadn't heard it herself! The security she depended on in their deep love for each other was a bewildering and shattering disappointment.

God frowned and slowly turned away from Adam. He knew what was going on in Adam's heart, but it had to be spoken aloud and displayed openly for it to be judged. It clearly wasn't the heartfelt sorrow of a contrite heart before an all-knowing God and He wanted Adam to realize it.

Adam had blamed God and Eve before admitting his own guilt. How appalling! Father's warnings to be totally honest with Him and to trust and honor Him seemed to have had no effect. Adam had a choice and he used it to make Eve accountable first, but to blame God too was the most disparaging act! It was disgusting! His commitment to Father had been thrown away quickly and carelessly, without a second thought, like a useless twig, totally valueless.

The promises between him and God were now regarded with little significance. He didn't consider he was breaking away from God by nullifying their agreement and he didn't seem to care that it left him vulnerable without Him. His only thought was to keep Eve.

If only he would admit his responsibility for what he had done, respect his commitment and the relationship he had with Father, and ask forgiveness, God would listen. But Adam didn't, and God could no longer converse with him because of it.

God turned next to Eve, *"What have you done?"* Eve hesitated, remembering other times when she had felt uncomfortable on the inside—though not as horrifying as now—and how good she felt again when she talked to Father about it. She blurted out tearfully, "The serpent tricked me and I ate Your fruit!" [5]

She groveled like Adam on the ground in guilt at what she had done. Regret would have been a mild word to describe the depth of her despair, but she tried to extend her feelings to Father one last time. She was ashamed and desperately needed Him to say it was okay, that everything was alright again. Yet the words God needed to hear, she didn't say—I am sorry for what I did! Please forgive me!

Regret and shame weren't enough to receive forgiveness without those words and they were vitally important. [6] It discarded the agreement she and Adam had made with Him—to respect Him as God—and barred Him from forgiving her. Asking for forgiveness would have reverenced Him and expressed sorrow for losing the bond she had with Him. But all Eve felt was fear of repercussions for herself and Adam because they had been caught in the act of disobedience.

Fearing God without asking forgiveness added to the insult and alienation of Him. Just like Adam, she didn't respect or value her relationship to Him. It was almost as if she never knew Him.

Neither human had ever experienced Father's anger. All they knew was His love and nothing of His justice. It was this love and mercy that Eve was searching for. She had correctly put the blame where it was due. She had said the truth and admitted to disobeying Him. A tinge of light remained on her.

But admitting her deed without asking for forgiveness was an incomplete attempt to be totally right with Him. It disregarded her commitment to Him and cut the bond she had with Him. She withdrew from Him, just like Adam did. She didn't take into account His words that if they got into trouble, He would set things right if only they would be honest, turn to Him in true humility, and reverence Him. All she and Adam felt was fear and distrust in their loving Father as a result of Satan's influence on them, even in that short time spent with him.

Though the opportunity still remained for them to express their sorrow and ask for forgiveness and help, they were allowing fear to overtake their faith in Father. It drained all they knew of God out of them and left them helpless, fumbling, and weak.

God turned to the serpent now with great anger and His voice rose in volume as He seethed in a fierce rage. The black storm clouds that had been brewing about now gathered about Him and His voice roared like a lion's, shaking the earth. Smoke churned around Him and He breathed out a sheet of devouring fire. [7]

> "Because you have done this, I curse you to be lowlier than cattle.
> You shall be a lower life form than any creature you had hoped to rule.
> Upon your belly shall you forever crawl.
> You will lick the dust of the ground all the days of your life." [8]

As He spoke, the serpent's legs and wings gradually receded into his body and the beast writhed under the judgment. His laughter was gone now, and he wriggled in hate and contempt, but he was terrified too.

> "And I will put hostility and war between you and the woman,
> and between your offspring and her son. [9]
> He shall crush your head—the authority you have stolen—

and obliterate you into a fiery eternity.
But you will only be able to bruise His heel." [10]

As the serpent's appendages withered, his tongue flicked in and out, tasting the ground around him. He wriggled hastily off the rock and slithered away in the underbrush.

Slowly God turned to Adam and Eve and His countenance softened. He fastened His attention on them in utter sadness for a long time as they tried to crunch themselves into the ground in shame. He thought again of all the hurt, not only for them, but for the many generations to come, and though He had a plan in place, it nevertheless deeply grieved Him to think of the suffering to come.

He spoke to Eve first as she awaited His pronouncement in torment.

"When you conceive, it will be with multiple sorrows.
In pain you shall bring children forth,
and your heart will break for your children
Your desire will turn only to your husband to lead you now.
He shall rule over you, dominate you, and abuse your faithfulness. [11]
It will be very difficult for him to hear Me because he chose to listen to you, and it will cause you much grief."

To Adam He said:

"Because you listened to your wife and disregarded Me,
and ate fruit from the tree which I commanded you not to do,
hereafter you will have great difficulty hearing from Me,
and the earth is cursed explicitly for you.
With much hard work and long hours
will you eke out whatever it provides for the rest of your life.
Only weeds, thorns, and thistles shall it produce for you.
You will have no choice but to eat it or starve. [12]
You have never known heavy toil, but now you will be a slave to the land,

sweating and straining to provide bread for your family
until your body is worn out and returns to the dirt.
For out of the dirt your body was made
and back to the ground it will return.
For dust you are, and to dust you shall return. (13)

It was a heavy sentence for them both and fell on them like a crushing blow. His words weren't announcements of retribution for what they had done, but consequences of their disobedience. He continued, *"Animals will fear you now. You will eat them when you have no food like you eat fruits and herbs."* (14)

He added to their misery with one final declaration, *"These curses will be passed on to your descendants because you have brought your seed with you into Satan's kingdom.* (15) *They will suffer the same consequences as you. Such is the life of bondage to Satan."* (16)

They lay feebly before him, wailing in horror, cringing, and trying to shrink away. And yet He held them with His gaze and a look on His face they didn't comprehend. It was an earnest expression and caused them to freeze at the first sign of hope they could detect.

XVIII. HOPE

Cast away from you all the transgression
which you have committed, and get your-
selves a new heart and a new spirit. For why
should you die? ... For I have no pleasure in
the death of one who dies, says the Lord God.
Therefore, turn and live.

Ezekiel 18: 31, 32. New King James

The Spirit was talking to Adam and Eve now. *"Be silent in the
presence of Father God, for He has prepared a way to help you.*
[1] *He has said He will put hostility and war between that snake,
the devil, and the woman, and between his offspring and hers.
God will use His word and the woman will have a son who will
save you and your children."* [2]

For the first time, Adam and Eve stopped wailing and
groveling to listen to the Spirit and they began to understand
that God had an alternative to their dilemma using Eve's son

and it would involve war between that son and the devil. Could they still be forgiven? If so, what would they have to do?

Maybe God wouldn't condemn Eve because she had been deceived when tempted, but Adam wasn't. [3] Would God separate Eve from Adam to have this special son? Adam couldn't conceive of living without her! Would God forgive her and not him? He had become a sinner for her sake. Would she forsake him now because he had blamed her? Adam couldn't discern her thoughts anymore, but he refused to live without her.

For Eve, her total concentration had been to have a family with Adam. How could that be possible without him? She had to be with him no matter what happened! She didn't realize what a profound difference it was going to make when Adam would become the only leader in her life without God. Or that God could easily create another partner for her if she was the one who asked forgiveness and turned away from Satan. Her heart hadn't considered it because she had already forsaken God for Adam.

She and Adam clung to each other as again the decision was made that day for one human to stay with the other without any thought to the higher consequence of living without God. The curse was already in effect—to stay with another one instead of God by disregarding Him, the most important person in their relationship. [4] There was no attempt to ask His forgiveness nor grieve over their lost tie to Him. Though they were sorrowful, it nevertheless remained a stance of pride for them to think they could endure without Him, and God hated it. This was the pride He had warned them about—the same pride that overtook Satan.

The look on God's face was determined as He stood in front of the Tree of Life and slowly took a step aside, revealing the two lambs that had romped alongside them earlier in the day. They now lay motionless at the base of the tree with blood oozing all around their lifeless little bodies. Their dainty pink mouths were gaped open in a silent scream and their eyes were open, unblinking, and blank. The life force within them was obviously gone. It was a shockingly gruesome scene for the couple to see these two innocent lambs that had played joyfully just hours before, but now suddenly dead.

"*This is the sacrifice provided for your guilt, one for each of you. Remember I said you would surely die the day you ate the fruit from My tree? I can transfer that punishment to something else to save you from total death. Death is not My way.* (5) *It is Satan's way when you fall into his hands. Now that you have obeyed him, you will live by his rules.*"

Father looked directly into their eyes as He offered the alternative. "*But if you are honest and turn away from your transgressions to Me, your punishment can be put on another living being that belongs to you. It can be offered in place of you and I can justifiably accept it—for now. In this way you can be temporarily restored to Me.*

"*But because you have given your earthly authority to Satan, things will be done his way. I can only intervene when you turn away from him, abandon your own independent decisions, look to Me with a contrite heart, accept My direction, and believe what I say. That will open the pathway between you and I again.*" After a pause He added, "*Teach this also to your children.*"

There was a hissing interruption in the air. "Don't listen to Him! He is wrong! He will cause all your misfortunes to come! He doesn't really care about you! You don't need Him anymore! The power to sustain you lies from within you. You can live without Him!" This came from the shadows with an evil vehemence.

God disregarded it and bent over the still bodies of the lambs. Quickly He peeled the skin away from their flesh with His own hands. Blood was everywhere including on His hands and feet and running in rivulets at the base of the Tree of Life. It spread on the ground and lay in spattered puddles while flies began buzzing around it—the first sign of feeding on dead carcasses. Then He fastened the moist, bloody side of the skins to Adam and Eve's bodies with the white fleece facing out, and they had their first lesson for making clothing. (6)

He was beginning to resemble more and more the angel who had talked to them before, but Adam and Eve paid little attention. *"There!"*, He said. *"You now live in a physical world."*

But He was also taking part in their world with the blood of the lambs on His hands and feet and pooling beneath Him at the base of the Tree of Life. To see Almighty God, creator of the universe, standing with the blood of the lambs on Him and all around Him was almost unfathomable!

Though they hadn't requested it, He was extending His mercy to them one last time and showing the way out of their disaster. He wanted to implant solidly in their minds a picture of the sacrifice it would take to save them. It needed to make an impression they would never forget.

His sadness was unmistakable as He presented the final detail. *"Don't forget Me or My words.*

I will place them in your mind and heart and you must write what happened here to pass on to your children. Tell them about Me. I am the Lord, full of compassion and mercy. I am slow to anger and filled with lovingkindness and faithfulness. I lavish unfailing love to thousands of generations. I forgive inequity, rebellion, and offences. (7)

"Don't forget ... My words ... Don't forget ... My love ...". Like a vapor, He was fast fading in front of them until He was gone.

They stood aghast at the suddenness of all these events. What would happen now? Was He gone forever? They felt agonizingly alone! Worse yet, would they also die like the lambs?

They embraced and sobbed with overwhelming loneliness and despair. Then Adam gasped and pulled away from Eve. For the first time he saw the spark of life on her, not as vibrant as usual, but it was definitely there. He checked his own body, but his glorious light was gone, and he grappled with the reason why there was a difference.

In his heart he knew. He still felt the dirtiness of his violation. He hadn't been entirely honest with God and that made a difference. He was aware of what he was doing when he ate the fruit, but Eve was deceived and spoke the truth about what she had done when he tried to hide it. [8]

How could he confess what he did to God? It put him wholly at fault when he had been entrusted to care for Eve as well as Eden and he couldn't bear the guilt. Why, oh why, hadn't he done away with Satan before?! Why hadn't he protected her and stood boldly against the usurper? Too late he remembered the warnings from God and he groaned in remorse.

Yet here was his bedraggled Eve standing there, still devoted to him, fidgeting anxiously. Her pale skin was still creamy white with a touch of radiance about her head. The lamb skin hung limply on her body, spattering her with blood and disgustingly ugly in contrast to the light of her former glory. He was brimming over with thankfulness for her!

They would start all over again, just the two of them. They would always have each other. He needed to reassure her first and taking her hand, he pressed it to his chest, dedicating his life to her. "I made a mistake, but I do love you and will never leave you. I commit myself to you from now on and forevermore. You, Eve, are my partner for life, and you truly will be the mother of all mankind and also be the mother of those who will live holy lives. [9] Our release from this kingdom of Satan's will come through your son who will be honest, just like you. He will win back our life with God once again."

Adam comprehended correctly that there was hope yet and all was not lost. Surely the curses that were placed on them couldn't be passed on to all their descendants! God had demonstrated that an innocent animal, such as a lamb, had to be killed and offered to God to renew the relationship he and Eve had with Him. It would represent them and be a substitute for their punishment. They were to teach this to their children until that special son was born.

But the concept of killing an innocent animal was repugnant and difficult for Adam to immediately accept. It was so completely against his nature. With resignation he surmised, "I must do it. I must learn how to kill animals and be good at it, not only to offer them to God, but to feed us when food is scarce, as Father has said." Then, "I will take good care you and our family until that son is born."

What he didn't comprehend was the woman God spoke about wasn't Eve, nor that the promised son wouldn't be born for centuries. Adam only understood there would be a son who would rescue them and it was the only hope he had. That hope would sustain him for the rest of his life.

Darkness quickly covered them both.

XIX. The Plan

God sat on His throne in heaven with His robes billowing around him, now sparkling clean and regal again. Myriads of attending angels flew about the throne with Michael and Gabriel standing at its foot.

With His Son beside Him, Father evaluated once more their plan for earth. The world They had created was never meant to hold tragedy and suffering. Yet each knew previously—before the world was even created—what Adam and Eve would do and how it would affect all of them. They knew that mankind's authority and power would be distorted through the deliberate strategies of Satan. What had happened was not a surprise.

But They had predetermined a strategy before creating the human race about how to rectify the impending path of doom. However, the timing and actions of Adam and Eve had to be played out first as well as Their own actions in order to have the family They so desired. This had to happen, and They discussed it again before putting their plan in motion.

"One alternative I had considered was to completely destroy the world and start all over again," Father told His son. "If it weren't for You, I would have lost Adam and Eve and all their descendants. But I couldn't deny My word to them. Also, there are the billions of faithful people in the future who will honor and trust Me, and I couldn't deny them either."

"We will win back the world to what We had originally planned," His son replied," but it will take time. Our plan has always been to enlarge Eden so it covers the world with abundant life where creatures and people never die. We will be in control again and the earth will never be overused or overpopulated. Until then, We will wait for Our immediate plan to be fulfilled."

Regardless of their foreknowledge and resolution, They both felt the loss deeply. It had cost dearly to create Adam and Eve, but having children was worth it. God's constant, overwhelming love had to be expressed, even to people that hadn't been born yet. (1)

"The new plan will not fail!" Father declared with firm determination. He directed a command to Gabriel, "Set in place a veil between mankind and Me. They won't be able to see My face anymore. The veil will separate them from Me and they won't see or hear Me as they did before. This will protect them from My just wrath. It will also set them apart from all the angels and they won't be able to see them either." (2) He motioned to Gabriel and off he flew in obedience.

Then, "Behold, the man has become like one of Us, to know evil as well as good. What if he also eats fruit from the Tree of Life and his body as well as his soul lives on forever? (3) He would live continually separated from Us and Satan would torment him with no end in sight."

The son commanded Michael, "Banish the man from Eden and set your mightiest guard at the entrance with a fiery sword flashing back and forth to prevent him from returning and eating from the Tree of Life. He must leave immediately!" (4) Michael flew off in an instant with the mission.

Father then addressed what was to become of Eve. "*The woman spoke the truth and My son will do likewise. Therefore, she will have an openness to Us that the man will struggle with because he listened only to her and didn't regard My words. So his heart will be darkened.* (5) *But she will follow him willingly and also leave the garden. This must happen, for though she was deceived by Satan, she has willingly chosen Adam as her only lord, and I can no longer help her. I can't abide either her corruption or Adam's in My presence, for I am holy.*

"*But I have reserved a future woman whose appearance is hidden until the time is right and she will have My son. She will keep Me as her lord and obey My Spirit. It will be a great mystery. I will hide it so none will know how and when it will happen.*"

The son added to their plan. "*After the sacrifice has been consummated, We will bring Our children to heaven when their time on earth is done. They will no longer contend with worldly temptations and Satan. They will be innocent before Us with pure minds and hearts yet again!*"

He commanded the angels, "*Start building homes in heaven like the ones Adam and Eve constructed for their family. Build them precisely according to the desire of each one of our children and when they join Us here, their homes will be waiting for them.* (6) *What joy We will have then!*"

Father continued, "*We will live among them in perfect peace again, as We have always planned. Despite all his devices, Satan won't understand this plan and won't be able to stop it.*"

Father and son reflected again about what their enemy had done and conferred together with disgusted anger about it. As one, they spoke of it. "*How We abhor sin and what it will do to people! It will distort the world. Death will have its way now and will expand into Eden, destroying it. All communication between life forms will wither away. There will only be survival of the strongest and there will be gruesome struggles between beasts as well as people to survive. Decay will be rampant as everything grows old.* [(7)] *The earth will mourn and all creation will be subject to futility along with mankind until We come back in full power.* [(8)]

They continued as one with the same thoughts. *"We made mankind to be spiritual beings connected to Us, but now they won't be able to see into the spirit realm.* [(9)] *Satan will play on that and entice them to look elsewhere for spiritual life. They will be drawn to his demons who will disguise themselves as angels, just like Satan disguised himself. Or demons will disguise themselves as dead relatives or friends who are familiar to those who are living.* [(10)] *They will speak to people and those who listen will be excited to be in contact with spirits, but it won't be Our Spirit of holiness. It will doom everyone who aligns himself with demons.*

"In their deception, people will turn to animals and waters and luminaries in the skies and other forms of nature and worship them instead of Us. They will be especially attracted to dragons, a symbol of their new father. They will make trinkets, objects, and statues out of wood and stone and metal and depend on them for help instead of Us. They will think their own craftsmanship makes them holy. They will also turn to dead ancestors and other people and pray to them instead of us. They will turn to their leaders or anyone they admire and set them up as their idols ... or look to themselves to be their own gods. They will depend on their "inner self" as their saving power, but they are blank in their spirits without Us and they will feel the desperation there. [(11)]

"They won't know We are jealous of idols and will tolerate none other in the lives of those who look to Us for help. Worse yet, they will keep their burdensome crimes and try to combine it with a relationship to Us without asking forgiveness or considering Our justice."

Then Father spoke a decree. *"Yet I am all powerful, even on earth! I created it and it belongs to Me! I will reign through My children without taking away their free will when they willingly come to Me through My Son. I will answer anyone who calls out to Me with a contrite heart and be with them and restore all that Satan has stolen. I can do exceedingly, abundantly more than they can ask or imagine and I will do it through My beloved Son."* (12)

At this, Father God glowed with pride as He gazed at His Son in admiration and approval. *"My Son is My own heart. He is a Son who is the same as Me. He will obey Me, and yet He will be the Son of mankind. We will spend much time together ...,"* His voice broke here and He wept with much sorrow, for this was His only son until His future family could be born, and the suffering the son would endure was heart wrenching. (13)

He reached out and touched His son on the chest. *"Behold, I impart a seal of love upon You, for love is as strong as death. Satan's jealousy is as cruel as a flame of the grave. It's a most vehement flame that will overwhelm the people and greet them in Satan's final abode unless love compels them back to Me."* (14)

He paused then and turned to look back down on earth. *"Behold, the people and their wails of torment!"* He was viewing future generations of people who would undergo the bondage of Satan and his demons. *"I am zealous for them to come and live safely with Me! For surely, they will be drawn to evil just like Adam and suffer greatly. Only love can save them now and it must be a strong love, a love that entails an excruciating death they can't ignore. It will be a death upon a tree instead of the Tree of Knowledge of Good and Evil that they lusted after. It will be a sacrifice so great that they will have to respect it, because by then, they will understand suffering.*

"They will have to acknowledge that death because after it is consummated, You will come alive again! No other person will conquer death like that! No idol, no person, no one! I will hold it up for all the world to see and it will be the most amazing feat when they see it! They won't be able to deny such a love as this—that You would lay down Your life and take such a great punishment for them—then overcome death just to rescue them! When Your body comes back to life, everyone will talk about it

because nothing like it has ever happened before. Then they will follow You and I can restore My fellowship with them, heal them, and bring them to My abode forevermore. (15)

His face brightened at the thought of this. *"The earth and all that it holds belongs to Us and We will restore it through our children once again. Our plan has never changed.* (16) *And You will win the crown of victory and be highly reverenced."*

But the son only thought about the souls He would win, not the glory. Father paused to consider His son. Then He merged His thoughts together with His son's until their minds became one and they tenderly embraced for a long time. As one person, they reflected again about the folly of future generations and how some would foolishly rebel against their plan to save them.

Father lamented at length as any parent would who has lost his children. *"My children, oh, My precious children! My heart cries out for you, My beloved ones! Will you let Me in your lives now? Will you listen to My words? No one can take your place! You have wrenched My heart because I know some of you will forsake Me! I see and know you already in the future and I miss you already! But I would birth you again just to have you back.* (17) *I would give all I have for you. I love you so! I always will love you, no matter what you do. I yearn exceedingly for you!"*

Then with a vengeance, Father addressed His enemy's tactics and in wrath He proclaimed, *"It is not over yet! I'll have them back! I did not come to destroy! For My people shall yet walk after their God. I shall roar like a lion at their enemy, but they will hear My voice, quiet and deep inside, and I will draw them gently to Me. They will follow Me alone. I have declared it!* (18) *It was their free will that got them in trouble, but I'll have them back through that same free will! For I am Lord of all!!!"*

XX. Aftermath

It was a beautiful evening for a Bible study, not too hot or too cold. The house shouldn't get overly warm like it usually did when friends came to fellowship and study the Bible together. The kids were engrossed in a special cartoon feature about super heroes on television.

Beth was busy with the dishes and trying to pray as she moved about the kitchen so she would be prepared for what God would do that night. But thoughts of what relishes and treats to put out for the company and last-minute room straightening kept interfering. "I should have the kids get that T.V. off," she mused, but she knew what a battle that would be. Anyway, it should be over in ten minutes. That's plenty of time, she thought.

She pondered for a moment about the cartoons her children seemed to be so intrigued with. They were always the same: flashy "demigod" characters who could fly through the air with unusual strengths and powers and who fought for "right". They could bend iron in their hands and fought with sinister adversaries who also had supernatural powers. The good guys wore bright outfits and always seemed to have lighter, more honest faces. The bad guys dressed in dark robes. They scowled with hate and had angry faces. Usually there was some type of wild animal that was their friend that also had super powers, either good—helping the good guys—or bad. The animals could talk and helped with whatever adventure was going on.

How ridiculous! Who could believe such garbage? She resented her children being captivated by programs like that. She didn't understand why they seemed so drawn to it and she felt it had a negative influence, but she would never be able to get them not to watch it.

For a brief moment she related the cartoons to a reoccurring dream she had been having. She was flying high and free, zooming high over the trees. Then she struggled to fly and something pulled her down at the end. "How ridiculous!" she thought again.

She wiped her hands and straightened her new blue outfit. "I sure hope Tom gets up in time," she thought. He had a couple of beers earlier and it always made him sleepy. It would be embarrassing if their friends arrived and her husband was still napping on the couch.

The TV program ended so she ordered the set off and reluctantly her children obeyed. Regular life was dull compared to the exciting life of superheroes with their super powers. The kids were always welcome to join the Bible study, but they had trouble getting involved after watching cartoons. Bible study was too boring, so they retired to their bedrooms.

She was looking forward to tonight and hummed a favorite hymn as she finished last minute preparations. She loved Bible studies ever since she had invited Jesus into her life. He took away all her addictions and she was ever so grateful, but it seemed she was continually dragging Tom along to these Bible meetings and church. She knew that not everyone, including Tom, was the same as her. Some took a long time to change, not wanting to completely give up the comfort and familiarity of their lifestyle. Their closeness to God seemed sporadic and weak, but she found it exhilarating.

"Kids, go wake your father before you hit the sack!" The dog hadn't been fed either and she quickly put food in his bowl. He looked at her quizzically before eating. "I swear," she thought, "when he looks at me that way, I think he is trying to tell me something." She commented absently to him, "I wish you could talk, Duke!"

Tom got off the couch just in time for the study and the weekly participants began pouring in, thirteen in all. She fluttered about them, welcoming each one, but Tom seemed not to care. Maybe he was just tired, but he always hung back a little. She wondered why it was so much harder for him to enjoy reading scripture in a group and she wished he would like it as much as she did.

Several men had brought guitars and a few women picked out the songs and began leading a chorus about God. As they sang, the little differences between them melted away and the group became one-minded as they worshiped. Each one truly loved God and it showed in their songs. When the guitars played slower, there was a new depth of feeling for Him coming from their hearts and they could sense His presence. It was so good to be with Him!

The songs ended, but the musicians were softly jamming, continuing the music, and everyone began praying. Beth felt a stirring inside and words began tumbling out with love for God. The group was praying to Him also, a little timidly, but gathering boldness as they discerned a new excitement in the room. They found themselves welcoming the Holy Spirit, though some really didn't know much about Him.

"Thank you, Father. Thank you for Your son. I am very thankful!" It seemed so right to tell Him this and when Beth felt His love pouring down on her, she prayed silently about her problems. "Lord, please help my husband. Make him spend more time with You." She peeked a glance at him. He was caught up in the reverent atmosphere and his eyes were closed, so she was reassured.

She had always noticed that the men seemed to have a more difficult time during this part of the study. It was the women who participated the most, although the men were getting better. She had been taught that men have too much pressure as leaders of their families and that was why they struggled. "But why are there always more women in church and gatherings like this than men?" she thought.

For a moment she contemplated the perplexity of men being aloof and struggling with hearing from God. Yet God had called them to be spiritual leaders of their families. "Why, Lord?", she asked silently. He must have a good reason. Tom had chided her on occasion, "You women need our discernment. Eve was the one who was deceived, not Adam", he would say. "Men protect the women from being gullible and getting into trouble."

The tempo of the music changed to a faster, happier beat. Beth continued to worship God quietly because Tom might say she "overdid it" if she was too loud, as if it embarrassed him. "I am thrilled to be here with you, my God," she prayed and relaxed a bit more. But she still questioned why husbands were so dominant with their wives. Were wives always supposed to submit to them, as she had been taught?

When the music was over, everyone paused for refreshments before they began the study. They were studying the eighth book of Proverbs. Each one read a paragraph and they discussed it as they went along.

"If anyone respects and fears God, he will hate evil. For wisdom hates pride, arrogance, corruption, and deceit of every kind." The reader droned on to the last paragraph. "Listen to My counsel. Oh! Don't refuse it—and be wise." He concluded with the last sentence, "... For whoever finds Me finds life and wins approval from the Lord. But the one who misses Me has injured himself irreparably. Those who refuse Me show that they love death."

She knew these scriptures were significant, but why was there so much emphasis on getting wisdom? She wished God would explain it plainly to her, but doubted that could ever happen. He didn't talk privately to people, or did He? She didn't believe God was boring, but sometimes she wished He would just talk to her!

They finished the chapter and each person shared how God's wisdom had changed their lives–how He had helped them and rescued them from potentially bad circumstances or healed them. Then they talked about the good things He had been doing lately.

One of them—a new Christian still excited about his recent experience with God—was particularly emphatic about his feeling for Him. "Knowing the Lord," he said, "how could anyone ever leave Him?"

Beth felt a tinge of smugness and thought, "He hasn't been a Christian long enough to know the pitfalls." The thought came quickly into her mind. "He'll see! We were all that crazy about God when we first became Christians too, but it wears off. There are so many other things to contend with and still remain a Christian, like sickness, money troubles, families in trouble, and other crisis people have to deal with. Life can be horrendous and it just goes on." She found herself wondering where these thoughts were coming from after such a grand time with God.

The meeting was concluding so they stood and Tom closed with a prayer. One of the ladies, Mary Ann, wanted prayer for her knee that had been hurting. The women flocked around her to pray, but since the group had prayed for it at a previous meeting, the men inwardly groaned with impatience and headed for a last-minute snack.

Beth extended her hand toward Mary Ann along with the others. "Father, we humbly ask You to heal this knee. We know You love Mary Ann. We ask this is Jesus's name." The women prayed a bit longer and Beth had sudden boldness. "I command the arthritis in this joint to leave right now. Knee, be healed!" She was exhilarated with this new courage and it felt right. The other ladies looked quizzically at her and she withdrew a little in embarrassment under their gaze, but Mary Ann said her knee felt somewhat better.

The meeting drew to an end and they all dispersed with hugs. Beth quietly picked up paper plates and used cups while Tom flicked on the T.V. and settled himself in his chair to watch the news. Absentmindedly Beth hummed one of the evening's tunes and bustled between the kitchen and living room. The kids were all in bed and Tom was in his own world with the television on.

"Glory, glory, to the Lamb", she hummed. "For You are glorious and worthy to be praised, the Lamb upon the throne!"

From his recliner, Tom complained, "Can you keep it down? I can hardly hear this!"

She wondered about how easily Tom could switch from being with God to watching the news. Deep in her heart she also ached for just a little respect. She resented the tone in his voice, and it irritated her. "He should respect me more. Maybe it would have been better if I hadn't married him." This thought came suddenly to her mind, startling her, but she thought about it only for a second.

She sighed with resignation because, "Compromise is needed sometimes to have peace in a marriage. Peace, after all, is God's way. Anyway, we love each other and I can't think of living without him. I just wish sometimes I could sit down and talk with him about these things, but he would never listen. Would it be against God's will to correct him? Would he ever change if I don't say something to him?"

A quiet new thought interrupted her chain of thinking. *"Don't be troubled. I am all you need. I formed you for Me."* [1] It

130

was a very subtle thought, but she knew it had to come from God because she would never think of it herself.

She continued with her work, but she was listening. *"I will bless your children if you teach them also."* Tears came to her eyes. How she ached to hear Him! Was it just her imagination? She had a strong feeling that He wanted to wipe away her tears. [2] She gulped and hurried on with her work. Ridiculous! I'm just tired, she thought, but she wanted to hear more.

"I desire you to spend more time with Me. Don't look to others who may hold you back. Follow Me. Choosing Me is choosing life."

She headed up the stairs for bed and fell exhausted on her pillow. The voice continued, *"I am also your husband. I have called you to be Mine and I will cover you with My peace.* [3]

"You shall correctly discern every thought and reject what is evil. [4] *Be honest with Me always, whatever is on your heart, and hide nothing. Don't you know I have already seen it?"*

She recalled her smugness earlier in the evening and she suddenly regretted it as well as her thoughts about Tom. "Lord, I'm sorry," she sighed. "Do You ever get tired of hearing my complaints about others?" She felt assurance inside and knew He heard her.

"There is no need for you to continue in the same way. There is nothing that separates us. Only what you choose to do."

She drifted off to sleep, very contented and secure, as if God Himself was standing guard over her. [5] But He was there, covering her with His warm blanket of grace. Was it a dream? She seemed to sense a peaceful presence.

"Trust My Word and follow Me first. Don't let anything or anyone take My place. I love you more than you can ever know. Don't forget ... My words ... don't forget ... I am with you always ..."

THE END

An afterthought ....

Some may consider this book's account of Adam and Eve as just an imaginary tale, but not all of it is fictional. God is real, though He can't be seen with the naked eye.

If we discard what He says about Adam and Eve in the Bible and look for more acceptable facts about the beginning of the human race, we discover finding the truth can be an endless journey that changes with time.

However, some historical findings point to evidence that Eden was a real place, even while mysteries and speculations continue to surround it. Ancient texts sometimes referred to it as the Delightful Garden of God. Archeological discoveries as well as scripture place it in the southwest land of ancient Mesopotamia. It was close to that area where ancient archeology finds were discovered in abundance. Some were artifacts containing inscriptions about the first man and woman as well as depictions with astounding similarities to Adam and Eve. [1]

Science has also suggested that there is a possibility that the mtDNA identity in women of every race can be traced back to one woman, though it's a complex and complicated ongoing study. Yet it hints that one man and one woman started the human race.

One truth that never changes, and that we are all aware of, is our own mistakes in life, just like Adam and Eve experienced.

We wonder what God thinks about our sins and speculate what He thinks about us. We have created different religions to satisfy that wondering, which often lead to a belief in a judgement of some kind. Or we don't admit our own disconnection to God and concoct the idea that all the power we need is within us. We don't need God. There is little interest in Him, until a crisis happens. It's also easy to blame Him for the tragedies that happen and wonder why He allows it, which complicates our relationship to Him.

Inevitably we look to the supernatural to find answers and intuitively we are drawn to God that way. Yet it can't be certain what is real in a world outside of our own physical norms. Jesus came back to life after being dead for three days and that is definitely a supernatural event, but it is also an historical fact, proven even beyond the testimonies in the Bible. [2]

Dying will be the most spiritual event we ever experience. How much do we really know will happen after we depart this life? What is God telling us about it? We can't make up our own fantasies about what we think may happen just to sooth our minds. We need to get in touch with the real God to tell us the truth because our lives depend on it.

The footnotes in this book are here to speak to us what God is saying about it. He wants us to come to Him through our relationship with Jesus. Jesus is the key.

Fran Lynghaug

1) The most famous of these ancient artifacts are two seals, one called the "Temptation Seal" in the British Museum, and the other, the "Adam and Eve Seal" in the University Museum of Pennsylvania, dated around 3500 B.C. (Halley, page 68)
2) There are many accounts from those who saw Jesus physically alive after he died beyond those in the Bible.

Here are just two witnesses who were His enemies and who wrote reports about His death:

Official report of Caiaphas, the Jewish high priest who condemned Jesus to death, to the Sanhedrim concerning the resurrection of Jesus. Taken from *The Archko Volume or The Archeological Writings of the Sanhedrim & Talmuds of the Jews*, p. 119, 120.: Sanhedrim, 89. By Siphri II, 7.: "To You, Masters of Israel: ... I feel in duty bound to communicate to you some facts that have come to my knowledge ... A few days after the execution of Jesus of Nazareth, the report of his resurrection from the dead became so common that I found it necessary to investigate it,...I sent for Malkus, the captain of the royal city guard, who informed me he knew nothing personally, as he had placed Isham in command of the guard: but from what he could learn from the soldiers, the scene was awe- inspiring, and the report was so generally believed that it was useless to deny it. ... He said that all the soldiers he had conversed with were convinced that Jesus was resurrected by supernatural power and was still living, and that he was no human being, for the light and the angels and the dead that came out of the graves all went to prove that something had happened that never occurred on earth before ... I sent for the lieutenant, who gave a lengthy account of the occurrence that morning, ... From this I am convinced that something transcending the laws of nature took place ... I find it is useless to try to get any of the soldiers to deny it, ..." (Caiaphas then questioned John and Peter and the two women, Mary and Joanna, who witnessed the angels at the empty tomb and also had a conversation with Jesus after he was resurrected.) On p 125, 126, Caiaphas continues, "As he (Jesus) proposes to bring hundreds of witnesses to prove all he says ...—witnesses whose veracity cannot be doubted— and as I had heard many of these things before from different men ... and their testimony corroborates other evidence that I have from other sources, that convinces me that this should not be rashly delt with ... besides, as John says, thousands of others equally strong in their belief, it throws me into great agitation. I feel some dreadful foreboding ... if I was mistaken, I was honest in my mistake. ... I shall try to clear myself of any charge, yet there is a conscious fear about my heart, so that I have no rest day or night. ... In this state of conscious dread, I remained investigating the Scriptures to know more about the prophecies concerning this man, ... I locked my door (to investigate the scriptures) ... when I lifted my eyes, behold, Jesus of Nazareth stood before me ..." (Caiaphas then records what Jesus said to him and continues.) "I fell on my face at his feet as one that was dead. When Annas lifted me up Jesus was gone, and the door still locked. None one could tell when or where he went.

"So noble Masters, I do not feel that I can officiate as priest any more. If this strange personage is from God, and should prove to be the Savior we have looked for so long, and I have been the means of crucifying him, I have no further offerings to make for sin; ..."

Pontius Pilot's report to Caesar on the arrest, trial, and crucifixion of Jesus, from *The Archko Volume or The Archeological Writings of the Sanhedrim & Talmuds of the Jews*, p. 138 - 147,: To Tiberius Caesar, Emperor of Rome. "*Noble Sovereign, Greeting*: The events of the last few days in my province have been of such a character that I will give the details in full as they occurred, ... Jesus was dragged before the High Priest, Caiaphas, and was sentenced to death. ... He sent his prisoner to me to confirm his condemnation and secure his execution. I answered him that, as Jesus was a Galilean, the affair came under Herod's jurisdiction and ordered him to be brought thither. The wily tetrarch ... committed the fate of the man to my hands. The Nazarene was brought back to me. ... 'Crucify him! Crucify him!' cried the relentless rabble. The vociferates of the infuriated mob shook the palace to its foundations.

135

"There was but one who appeared to be calm in the midst of the vast multitude: it was the Nazarene.... I then ordered Jesus to be scourged, ... I then called for a basin, and washed my hands ... thus testifying that in my judgment Jesus of Nazareth had done nothing deserving of death; but in vain. It was his life these wretches thirsted for. ... (Then) The crowed appeared not to walk, but to be borne off from the portals of the praetorium even unto Mount Zion, ... I ... contemplated athwart the deary gloom these fiends of Tartarus dragging to execution the innocent Nazarene. ... (Then) So dreadful were the signs that men saw both in the heavens and on the earth that Dionysius the Aeropagite is reported to have exclaimed... 'Either the author of nature is suffering or the universe is falling apart.' Whilst these appalling scenes of nature were transpiring, there was a dreadful earthquake ... Near the first hour of the night I ... went down into the city toward the gates of Golgotha. The sacrifice was consummated. ... I returned to the praetorium, ... As I am told that Jesus taught a resurrection and a separation after death, (Joseph of Arimathea asked) ... permission to bury Jesus of Nazareth.' 'Your prayer is granted,' said I to him; ... Joseph buried Jesus in his own tomb. ... The day after he was buried one of the priests came ... and said they were apprehensive that his disciples intended to steal the body of Jesus and hide it, and then make it appear that he had risen from the dead, as he had foretold ... I sent him to the captain of the royal guard (Malcus) to tell him to take the Jewish soldiers, place as many around the sepulchre as were needed; ... (Later) When the great excitement arose about the sepulchre being found empty, ... I sent for Malcus, who told me he had placed ... one hundred soldiers around the sepulchre ...and the soldiers were very much alarmed at what had occurred there that morning. ... at about the beginning of the fourth watch they saw a soft and beautiful light over the sepulchre, ...the whole place was lighted up, and there seemed to be crowds of the dead in their graveclothes. ... and the most beautiful music he had ever heard; and the whole air seemed to be full of voices praising God. ... I asked him if he had been questioned by the priests. He said he had. They wanted him to say it was an earthquake, and that they were asleep, and offered him money to say that the disciples came and stole Jesus; but he saw no disciples. ... He said that some of (the priests) thought that Jesus was no man; that he was not a human being; that he was ... (like) the same persons had been on the earth before with Abraham and Lot, and at many times and places. ... if the Jewish theory be true, these conclusions are correct, for they are in accord with this man's life, as is known and testified by both friends and foes, ...; he could change death into life, disease into health; he could calm the seas, still the storms, ... Now I say, if he could do all these things, which he did, and many more, as the Jews all testify, ... and all these facts are known to thousands, as well by his foes as by his friends—I am almost ready to say, as did Manlius at the cross, 'Truly this was the Son of God.' Now, noble Sovereign, this is as near the facts in the case as I can arrive at, ... I am your most obedient servant, "Pontius Pilate."

FOOTNOTES

(God's stepping stones to Him)

Bible translations used in footnote references:

KJ - King James   LB - Living Bible

NKJ - New King James   NLT - New Living Translation

CHAPTER 1. EVE

1) You have ravished my heart, my sister, my spouse, you have ravished my heart, with one look of your eyes ... Song 4:9 NKJ

2) ... for thou hast created all things and for thy pleasure they are and were created. Rv. 4:11 KJ

3) ... the children of Israel could not look steadily at the face of Moses because of the glory of his countenance. ... For as he gave them God's law to obey, his face shone out with the very glory of God ... 2 Cor. 3: 7 NKJ

The light of the righteous rejoices ... Pr. 13:9 NKJ
As He was praying, His face began to shine, and His clothes became dazzling white and blazed with light. Luke 9:29 LB
4) For the earth bringeth forth fruit of herself. ... Mark 4:28 KJ
5) ... He blessed them and then began rising into the sky, and went on to heaven. Luke 24:51 LB
... and when they were come up out of the water, the Spirit of the Lord caught away Philip, that the eunuch saw him no more. Acts 8:39 NKJ
6) And the cow and the bear shall graze; their young ones shall lie down together: and the lion shall eat straw like the ox ... They shall not hurt nor destroy in all My holy mountain. Isa. 11:6 -9 NKJ. [Archaeologists have identified populations of leopards and bears dating from prehistory in southeast Iran. Taken from ARCHAEOLOGY, A publication of the Archaeological Institute of America. Sept/Oct. 2020, p.16.]
7) ... her barren wilderness will become as beautiful as the Garden of Eden. Joy and gladness will be found there, thanksgiving and lovely songs. Is. 51:3 LB
8) I will make your towers of sparkling agate and your gates and walls of shining gems. Is. 54:12 LB
And He built His sanctuary like high palaces, like the earth which He hath established forever. Ps. 78:69 KJ
9) The name of the first (river in Eden) is Pison: that is it which compasseth the whole land of Havilah where is gold: And the gold in that land is good: ... Gen. 2:11, 12 KJ
The foundations of the wall of the city were adorned with all kinds of precious stones, ... And the street of the city was pure gold, like transparent glass. Rv. 21:19 – 21 NKJ
10) ... the whole procession began to shout and sing ... praising God ... But some of the Pharisees ... said, "Sir, rebuke your followers ... !" He replied, "If they keep quiet, the stones along the road will burst into cheers!" Luke 19:37- 40 LB

CHAPTER 2. ADAM
1) God is the Lord. He has given us light. Ps. 118:27 NKJ
... you are light in the Lord. Walk as children of light ... Eph. 5:8 NKJ

... become blameless and harmless, children of God ... among whom you shine as lights in the world. Phil. 2:15 NKJ

2) Definitions for the name Adam: "flush, rosy, or ruddy", possibly indicating the color of earth he was made from. Strong's Exhaustive Concordance of the Bible, Dictionary of the Hebrew Bible, p. 8, # 119 and 122.

3) ... For an angel of the Lord came down from heaven ... His face shone like lightening and his clothing was a brilliant white. Matt. 28:2, 3 LB

4) But Jesus knew their thoughts ... Matt.12:25 LB

5) ... God said, "it isn't good for man to be alone; I will make a companion for him, a helper ... So the Lord God formed ... every kind of animal and brought them to the man ... But still there was no proper helper for the man. Gen. 2:18 - 20 LB

6) Then the rib which the Lord God had taken from the man He made into a woman, and He brought her to the man. And Adam said, "... She shall be called Woman because she was taken out of Man." Gen. 2: 22, 23 NKJ

CHAPTER 3. AN UNHOLY PLACE

1) By faith, Enoch was translated ... Heb.11:5 KJ
Then the Spirit lifted me up ... So the Spirit lifted me up and took me away ... Ezekiel 3:12, 14 NKJ
He blessed them and then began rising into the sky, and went on to heaven. Luke 24:51 LB
... and when they were come up out of the water, the Spirit of the Lord caught away Philip, that the eunuch saw him no more. Acts 8:39 NKJ
... And the first voice, which I heard ... saying ... "Come up here..." Immediately I was in the Spirit; and behold, a throne set in heaven, and One sat on the throne. Rv. 4:1, 2 NKJ
So the angel took me in spirit into the wilderness ...
Rv. 17:3 LB

CHAPTER 4. THE SPIRIT

1) And I remind you of those angels who were once pure and holy, but turned to a life of sin ... Jude 6 LB

FOOTNOTES

For if the Lord spared not the angels who sinned, but cast them down ... 2 Pet. 4 NKJ

2) When they passed the first and second guard posts, they came to the iron gate that leads to the city, which opened to them of its own accord, and they went out and down one street ... Acts 12:10 NKJ

CHAPTER 5. SATAN

1) ... the Lord will ... punish leviathan, the swiftly moving serpent, the coiling, writhing serpent, the dragon of the sea* ... Isaiah 27:1 LB (* "sea" may represent many people)
2) Is. 14:13 LB
3) And the dragon was enraged with the woman, and he went to make war with the rest of her offspring ... Rv. 12:17 NKJ
4) ... So they worshipped the dragon ... Rv. 13:4 NKJ
5) His eyes glow like sparks. Fire leaps from his mouth. Smoke flows from his nostrils, like steam from a boiling pot ... When he stands up, the strongest are afraid. Terror grips them. Job 41: 20,25 LB

CHAPTER 6. FATHER GOD

1) ... a whirlwind was coming out of the north, a great cloud with raging fire engulfing itself; and brightness was all around it and radiating out of its midst like the color of amber, out of the midst of the fire. Ezekiel 1:4 NKJ
... And the Ancient of Days was seated; His garment was white as snow, and the hair of His head was like pure wool. His throne was a fiery flame ... A thousand thousands ministered to Him ... Da. 7:9, 10 NKJ
... behold, a throne set in heaven, and One sat on the throne. And He who sat there was like a jasper and a sardius stone in appearance ... And from the throne proceeded lightnings, thunderings, and voices ... Rv. 4:2, 3, 5 NKJ
... the temple of God was opened ... And there were lightnings, noises, thunderings, an earthquake, and great hail. Rv. 11:19 NKJ
2) For our God is a consuming fire. Heb. 12:29 LB
God is light and in Him is no darkness at all. 1 John 1:5 NKJ

141

3) ... And I heard the sound of harpists playing their harps ...
    Rv. 14: 2 NKJ
    Then I looked, and I heard the voice of many angels around
    the throne ... and the number of them was ten thousand
    times ten thousand, and thousands of thousands ...
    Rv. 5:11 NKJ
4) And the angel ... said to him, "I am Gabriel, who stands in
    the presence of God, ... Luke 1: 19 NKJ
5) ... All Your waves and billows have gone over me.
    Ps. 42:7 NKJ
6) Then God took the man and put him in the Garden of Eden
    to tend and keep it. [farm and protect it] Gen. 2:15 NKJ
7) "Call upon Me in the day of trouble; I will deliver you, and
    you shall glorify Me." Ps. 50:15 NKJ
8) Then God blessed them and God said to them, "... fill the
    earth and subdue it; have dominion over the fish of the sea,
    over the birds of the air, and over every living thing that
    moves on the earth." Gen. 1:28 NKJ
    And the Lord God commanded the man, saying, "Of every
    tree of the garden you may freely eat, but of the tree of the
    knowledge of good and evil you shall not eat."
    Gen 2:16, 17 NKJ
9) The heaven, even the heavens, are the Lord's; But the earth
    He has given to the children of men. Ps.115:16 NKJ
10) "... For I, the Lord your God, am a jealous God ..."
    Ex. 20:5 NKJ
11) ... they did not ask counsel of the Lord. Josh. 9:14 NKJ
    So I advise you to live according to your new life in the
    Holy Spirit ... Gal. 5:16 NLT
12) ... I have set before you life and death, blessing and cursing:
    therefore choose life that both you and your descendants
    may live. Deut. 30:19 NKJ
13) He made two cherubim of beaten gold...one cherub on one
    end (of the mercy seat) and the other cherub at the other
    end ...The cherubim spread out their wings ... they faced one
    another, the faces of the cherubim were toward the mercy
    seat. Ex. 37:7- 9 NKJ

Above the golden chest were statues of angels called the
cherubim – the guardians of God's glory – with their wings
stretched out over the ark's golden cover called the mercy
seat ... that is why the sacred tent (containing the ark) here
on earth and everything in it – (were) all copied from things
in heaven ... He. 9:5, 23 LB

14) But he spoke more vehemently, "If I have to die with You,
I will not deny You!" Mark 14:31 NKJ
15) ... And the Lord God will wipe away tears from all faces; ...
Is. 14: 13 LB
And God will wipe away all tears from their eyes ...
Rv. 21:4 NKJ
16) And He took them up in His arms, laid His hands on them,
and blessed them. Mark 10:16 NKJ
17) ... God is love. 1 John 4:8. ... (God) is full of compassion,
longsuffering, and abundant in mercy and truth.
Ps. 86:15 NKJ
"... for the Father Himself loves you ..." John 16:27 NKJ.
18) ... May the Lord's face radiate with joy because of you;
Nu. 6:25 LB

CHAPTER 7. CREATOR GOD

1) And Adam said, "This is now bone of my bones, and flesh
of my flesh." Gen.2:23 NKJ
2) So God created man in his own image, in the image of
God he created he him; male and female created he them.
Gen.1:27 KJ
3) And the Lord God said, "It isn't good for man to be alone;
I will make a companion for him, a helper suited to his
needs." So the Lord God formed from the soil every kind
of animal and bird, and brought them to the man ... But still
there was no proper helper for the man. Gen. 2:18-20 LB
4) ... The tree of life was also in the midst of the garden and
the tree of knowledge of good and evil. Gen. 2:9 NKJ
5) He made him (Jacob) ride in the heights of the earth ...
Deut. 32:13 NKJ
I know a man in Christ who ... was caught up to the third
heaven ... such a one was caught up to the third heaven ...

how he was caught up into Paradise and heard inexpressible words ... 2 Cor. 12: 2-5 NKJ

... and the Spirit lifted me up between earth and heaven ... Eze. 8:3 NKJ

6) A river from the land of Eden flowed through the garden to water it; afterwards the river divided into four branches ... The third branch is the Tigris ... and the fourth is the Euphrates. Gen. 2:10, 14 LB

7) (Later this would be called the Mediterranean Sea where it would expand after the earth was broken up with a future flood.)

... all the fountains of the great deep were broken up ... and the rain was on the earth forty days and forty nights. Gen. 7:11-12 NKJ

8) ... a mist went up from the earth and watered the whole face of the ground. Gen. 2:6 NKJ

9) Book of Enoch 18:1-4, 34:1-2, 41:3-5

10) In his goodness he chose to make us his own children by giving us his true word. And we, out of all creation became his choice possession. James 1:18 NLT

11) I drew them with gentle cords, with bands of love ... Hosea 11:4 NKJ

... thou hast possessed my reins ..." Ps. 139:13 KJ

... You have loosed my bonds. Ps.116:16 NKJ

The kings of the earth ... set themselves against the Lord and His anointed, saying, "Let us break Their bonds in pieces, and cast away Their cords from us." Ps 2:2, 3 NKJ.

Canst thou ... loose the bands of Orion? Job 38:31 KJ

Day unto day utters speech, and night unto night reveals knowledge. There is no speech nor language where their voice is not heard. Their line has gone out through all the earth, and their words to the end of the world. Ps. 19:2-4 NKJ

12) He existed before everything else began, and he holds all creation together. Col.1:17 NLT

13) "... the Holy Spirit ... shall guide you into all truth, for he will not be presenting his own ideas, but will be passing on to you what he has heard." John 16:13 LB

144

But we know about these things because God has sent His Spirit to tell us all of God's deepest secrets ... And no one can know God's thoughts except God's own Spirit.
1 Cor. 2:10, 11 LB

14) If an ox gores a man or woman to death, the ox shall be stoned and its flesh not eaten ... Ex. 21:28 LB
The wolf and the lamb shall feed together. The lion shall eat straw like the ox and dust shall be the serpent's food. They shall not hurt nor destroy in all My holy mountain, says the Lord. Is. 65:25 NKJ

15) God blessed them (the man and woman) and told them, "Multiply and fill the earth and subdue it...Be masters over ... all the animals." Gen. 1:28 NLT
Then the Lord planted a garden in Eden, in the east, and there he placed the man he had created. And the Lord God planted all sorts of trees in the garden-beautiful trees that produced delicious fruit... The Lord placed the man in the Garden of Eden to tend and care for it. Gen. 2:8,9, 15 NLT

CHAPTER 8. THE ANGEL

1) ... The decrees of the Lord are trustworthy making wise the simple ... giving insight to life ... each one is fair ... They are a great reward for those who obey them.
Ps.19: 7 - 9, 11 NLT

2) These (are the) proverbs ... to know wisdom and instruction, to perceive the words of understanding. Pr. 1:1 - 4 KJ

3) ... If you hear me calling and open the door, I will come in, and we will share a meal as friends. Rev. 4:20 NLT

4) For you are a holy people to the Lord your God, and the Lord has chosen you to be a people for Himself, a special treasure ... Deut.14:2 NKJ

5) Let Israel rejoice in their Maker: Let the children of Zion be joyful in their King. Ps. 149:2 NKJ
Let them praise His name with the dance ... Praise Him with the timbrel and dance. Ps. 149:2, 150:4 NKJ
Behold My servants shall sing for joy of heart.
Is. 65: 14 NKJ

... (The Lord) will rejoice over you with great gladness. ... He will exult over you by singing a happy song. Zeph. 3:17 NLT

6) Then I lay down and slept in peace and woke up safely, for the Lord was watching over me. Ps. 3:5 LB

CHAPTER 9. A WALK IN THE PARK

1) ... The mountains and the hills shall break forth into singing before you, And all the trees of the fields shall clap their hands. Is. 55:12 NKJ

   ... Let the field be joyful and all that is in it. Then all the trees of the woods will rejoice before the Lord. ... Let the rivers clap their hands; Let the hills be joyful together before the Lord ... Ps. 96:12, 98:8 NKJ

2) And God said, "See, I have given you every herb that yields seed which is on the face of all the earth, and every tree whose fruit yields seed; to you it shall be for food. Also to every beast of the earth, to every bird of the air, and to everything that creeps on the earth in which there is life, I have given every green herb for food, and it was so." Gen. 1:29-30 NKJ

3) The wolf also shall dwell with the lamb. The leopard shall lie down with the young goat. The calf and the young lion and the fatling together; And a little child shall lead them. The cow and the bear shall graze, their young ones shall lie down together, and the lion shall eat straw like the ox ... They shall not hurt nor destroy in all My holy mountain." (This was always God's will.) Is. 11:6, 7, 9 NKJ

4) So the donkey said to Balaam, "Am I not your donkey on which you have ridden, ever since I became yours, to this day? ..." [Animals speaking to people]. Nu.22:30 NKJ

5) "And look! I have given you the seed-bearing plants throughout the earth, and all the fruit trees for your food. And I have given all the grass and plants to the animals and birds for their food." Gen. 1:29, 30 LB

6) ... the devil having already put it into the heart of Judas Iscariot ... to betray Him ... John 13:2 NKJ

CHAPTER 10. LIVING AS ONE

1) And Samson...took hold of the doors of the gate of the city and the two gateposts, pulled them up, bar and all, put them on his shoulders, and carried them to the top of the hill ... Judges 16:3 NKJ

2) Blessed is the man that walketh not in the counsel of the ungodly, ...Ps 1:1 KJ

3) ... "Let each of you speak the truth with his neighbor," for we are members of one another. "Be angry and do not sin", do not let the sun go down on your wrath, nor give place to the devil. Eph. 4:25-27 NKJ

4) Love never fails. 1 Cor. 13:8 NKJ

CHAPTER 11. LUCIFER

1) You were the seal of perfection, Full of wisdom and perfect in beauty. ... You were the anointed cherub who covers, I established you; You were on the holy mountain of God; You walked back and forth in the midst of fiery stones. You were perfect in your ways from the day you were created; Till iniquity was found in you. Eze. 28:11, 14, 15 NKJ
Thou hast been in Eden the garden of God; every precious stone was thy covering ...; the workmanship of thy tabrets and of thy pipes was prepared in thee in the day that thou wast created. Eze. 28:13 KJ

2) By the abundance of your trading, [taking a portion of worship for himself] you became filled with violence within; And you sinned ... Your heart was lifted up because of your beauty; You corrupted your wisdom for the sake of your splendor; ... Eze. 28:16, 17 NKJ
For you have said in your heart: 'I will ascend into heaven. I will exalt my throne above the stars of God. I will also sit on the mount of the congregation, on the farthest side of the north: I will ascend above the heights of the clouds. I will be like the Most High.' Is.14:13, 14 NKJ

3) And He (Jesus) said to them, "I saw Satan fall like lightening from heaven." Luke 10:18 NKJ

4) Take a look at the behemoth!... See his powerful loins ...How ferocious he is among all of God's creations. The mountains

offer their best food to him-—the other wild animals on which he preys. Job 40:15, 16, 19 LB

5) Pride goes before destruction, and a haughty spirit before a fall. Pr. 16:18 NKJ

,,, Satan can change himself into an angel of light, so it's is no wonder his servants can do it too and seem like godly ministers. In the end they will get every bit of punishment their wicked deeds deserve. 2 Cor. 11:14 LB

6) Your pomp is brought down to Sheol, and the sound of your stringed instruments ... How you are fallen from heaven, O Lucifer, son of the morning! How you are cut down to the ground. You who weakened the nations! Is. 14:11, 12 NKJ

(In the Hebrew Bible, Sheol is a place of darkness to which the dead go, also called Hades.)

... therefore I will cast thee as profane out of the mountain of God; and I will destroy thee, O covering cherub, ... I will cast thee to the ground, I will lay thee before kings, that they may behold thee. ... therefore will I bring forth fire from the midst of thee. It shall devour thee, and I will bring thee to ashes upon the earth in the sight of all them that behold thee. Eze. 28:16-18 KJ

He laid hold of the dragon, that serpent of old, who is the Devil and Satan, and ... cast him into the bottomless pit... Rv. 20:2,3 NKJ

7) ... and God said unto them, "Be fruitful and multiply, and replenish the earth, and subdue it ..." Gen. 1: 28 KJ

And God said, "Behold, I have given you every herb bearing seed, which is upon the face of all the earth, and every tree in the which is the fruit of a tree yielding seed; to you it shall be for meat. Gen. 1:29 KJ

Then God said, Let the earth bring forth the living creature according to its kind ... and everything that creeps on the earth according to its kind. And God saw that it was good. Gen.1:24, 25 NKJ

8) For we are God's masterpiece. He has created us anew in Chirst Jesus, so that we can do the good things he planned for us long ago. Eph. 2:10 NLT

9) The heaven, even the heavens, are the Lord's; but the earth hath he given to the children of men. Ps. 115:16 KJ

10) "You are of your father, the devil, and the desires of your father you want to do. He was a murderer from the beginning and does not stand in the truth, because there is no truth in him. When he speaks a lie, he speaks from his own resources, for he is a liar and the father of it." (Jesus speaking to the Jews who believed Him and yet didn't follow Him.) John 8:44 NKJ

11) And the Lord God commanded the man, saying, "Of every tree of the garden you may freely eat, but of the tree of knowledge of good and evil you shall not eat, for in that day that you eat of it you shall surely die. Ge. 2:16 NKJ

12) "Oh, there is so much more I want to tell you, but you can't understand it now." (Jesus Christ) John 16:12 LB

CHAPTER 12. THE TREE

1) ... The mountains and the hills shall break forth into singing before you, and all the trees of the field shall clap their hands. Is. 55:12 NKJ

Let the heavens rejoice, and let the earth be glad, Let the sea roar, and all its fullness; Let the field be joyful, and all that is in it. Then all the trees of the woods will rejoice before the Lord. Ps. 96:11, 12 NKJ

Make a joyful shout to God, all the earth! ... All the earth shall worship You and sing praises to You: They shall sing praises to Your name. Ps.66:1, 4 NKJ

2) Let everything that has breath praise the Lord. Ps. 150:6 NKJ

3) I said you are gods, and all of you are children of the Most High. Ps. 82:6 NKJ

Jesus answered them, "Is it not written in your law, 'I said you are gods'"? John 10:35 KJ

4) Excerpt from the Ancient Book of Enoch, Ch. 32:3, 4

CHAPTER 13. THE TEST

1) ... For Satan himself transforms himself ... 2 Cor. 11:14 NKJ

2) Gen. 3:1-5 NKJ

3) She took of the fruit and ate. She also gave to her husband with her and he ate. Gen. 3:6 NKJ

CHAPTER 14. THE CURSE

1) Then the eyes of both of them were opened, and they knew that they were naked, and they sewed fig leaves together and made themselves coverings. Gen. 3:7 NKJ
2) "You are of your father the devil, and the desires of your father you want to do." (Jesus said to Jews who believed Him.) John 8:44 NKJ
3) The thief does not come except to kill, and to steal, and to destroy ... John 10:10 NKJ
   ... even the things of nature, like animals and plants, suffer in sickness and death ... Rom.8:22 LB

CHAPTER 15. IN THE THRONE ROOM

1) ...and behold, a ladder was set up on the earth, and the top of it reached to heaven; and behold the angels of God ascending and descending on it. Gen.28:12 KJ
   And the posts of the door were shaken by the voice of him who cried out, and the room was filled with smoke. Is. 6:4 NKJ
2) And behold, the Lord stood above (the ladder) ... And Jacob awaked out of his sleep, and he said, Surely the Lord is in this place; and I knew it not. And he was afraid and said, How dreadful is this place! This is none other than the house of God, and this is the gate of heaven. Gen.28:13, 16, 17 KJ
3) I saw the Lord sitting on a throne, high and lifted up, and the train of his robe filled the temple. Above it stood seraphim; each had six wings: with two he covered his face, with two he covered his feet, and with two he flew. And one cried to another and said, "Holy, holy, holy is the Lord of hosts; The whole earth is filled with His glory!" Is. 6:1, 2 NKJ
4) "...Go tell that fox, 'Behold, I cast out demons and perform cures ... '" Luke 13:32 NKJ
5) ... He groaned in the Spirit and was troubled...Then Jesus, again groaning in Himself ... John 11:33, 38 NKJ

"...How often I wanted to gather your children together, as a hen gathers her brood under her wings, but you were not willing! See! And your house is left to you desolate; ..." Luke 13:34 NKJ

6) My grief is beyond healing; my heart is broken. Listen to the weeping of my people ... "Where is the Lord?" they ask. "Has God deserted us?" Jer. 8:18, 19 LB
   For the hurt of the daughter of my people I am hurt. I am mourning ... Jer. 8:21 NKJ

7) For as the body without the spirit is dead, ... James 2:26 KJ

8) ... only by dying could he (Jesus) break the power of the Devil, who had the power of death. Only in this way could he deliver those who have lived all their lives as slaves to the fear of dying. Heb. 2:14,15 NLT

9) Then I heard again what sounded like the shouting of a huge crowd, or like the waves of a hundred oceans crashing on the shore, or like the mighty rolling of great thunder, ... Rv. 19:6 LB

10) ... The only begotten Son, who is in the bosom of the Father, has declared Him. ... John 1:18 NKJ
    I and My Father are one. ... the Father is in Me and I in Him. (Jesus Christ) John 10:30, 38 KJ
    Believe Me, I am in the Father and the Father (is) in Me, ... (Jesus Christ) John 14:11 NKJ

11) His head and hair were white like wool, as white as snow ...Rv.1:14 NKJ

12) Being born again, not of corruptible seed, but of incorruptible, by the word of God, ...1 Pet.1:23 KJ

13) Therefore, just as through one man, sin entered the world, and death through sin, and thus death spread to all men ... Rom. 5:12 NKJ

14) And the Lord God said to Moses, "Go, get down! For your people ... have corrupted themselves ... and I will make of you a great nation." Ex. 32:7, 10 NKJ [An example of why God would change His plan because of people sinning.]

CHAPTER 16. JUSTICE

1) Then Moses pleaded with the Lord his God and said, "Lord, why does Your wrath burn hot against your people ...?" Eze. 32:11 NKJ

2) ... For the Lord is a God of justice: ... Is. 30:18 NKJ

3) Then the devil ... showed Him all the kingdoms of the world in a moment of time. And the devil said to Him, "All this authority I will give to You, and their glory, for this has been delivered to me, and I give it to whomever I wish." Luke 4: 5, 6 NKJ

4) "... One mightier than I is coming, ... He will baptize you with the Holy Spirit and fire." Luke 3:16 NKJ
   I have come to bring fire to the earth, ... Luke 12:49 NLT

5) ... For the things which are seen are temporary, but the things which are not seen are eternal. 2 Cor. 4:18 NKJ

6) The thief does not come except to steal, to kill, and to destroy. I have come that they may have life, and that they may have it more abundantly. John 10:10 NKJ

7) [Father and Son are one, of the same heart, but are one plural being. ("... in the day that the Lord God made the earth ...") "Lord God" here in Genesis 2:4 is the Hebrew word 'elôhîym, which is specially used in the plural of the supreme God;] #430 of the Hebrew and Chaladee Dictionary, Strong's Exhaustive Concordance.)
   "... I came forth from God. I came forth from the Father ..." (Jesus Christ) John 16:27, 28 NKJ
   "... Whom shall I send? Who will go for Us?" Then I said, "Here am I. Send me." Is. 6:8 NKJ
   Long ago, even before He made the world, God loved us and chose us in Christ to be holy and without fault in His eyes. His unchanging plan has always been to adopt us into His own family by bringing us to Himself through Jesus Christ. And this gave Him great pleasure. Eph. 1:4, 5 NLT

8) ... and (he) fell on his (father's) neck and wept on his neck a good while. Gen. 46:29 NKJ

9) "... 'You are My Son. Today I have begotten You. Ask of Me, and I will give You the nations for Your inheritance, and the ends of the earth for Your possession. You shall break

them with a rod of iron: You shall dash them to pieces..."
Ps. 2:7 - 9 NKJ

10) "... For the Father judges no one, but has committed all judgement to the Son, that all should honor the Son just as they honor the Father ... he who hears My word and believes in Him who sent Me has everlasting life, and shall not come into judgement, but has passed from death to life." Jesus Christ. John 5:22 -24 NKJ

11) How can I give you up, Ephraim? How can I hand you over, Israel ... My heart churns within Me; My sympathy is stirred. Hosea 11:8 NKJ

12) When Jesus therefore saw her weeping, and the Jews also weeping ... He groaned in the Spirit and was troubled. ... Jesus wept. John 11:33, 35 KJ

13) And the Holy Spirit descended in bodily form like a dove upon Him, and a voice from heaven which said, "You are My beloved Son; in You I am well pleased," Luke 3:22 NKJ And a cloud came and overshadowed them; and a voice came out of the cloud, saying, "This is My beloved Son. Hear Him." Mark 9:7 NKJ
"Father, glorify Your name." Then a voice came from heaven saying "I have both glorified it and will glorify it again." ... Jesus answered and said, "This voice did not come because of Me, but for your sake..." John 12: 28, 30 NKJ

CHAPTER 17. CONSEQUENCES

1) ... Adam and his wife hid themselves from the presence of the Lord God among the trees of the garden. Gen.3:8 NKJ

2) Gen. 3:9 NKJ

3) Gen. 3:11 NKJ

5) Gen. 3:13 NKJ

6) For God can use sorrow in our lives to help us turn away from sin and seek salvation. We will never regret that kind of sorrow. But sorrow without repentance is the kind that results in death. 2 Cor. 7: 10 NKJ

7) Then the earth shook and trembled. The foundations of heaven quaked and were shaken. Because He was angry,

smoke went up from His nostrils, and devouring fire from His mouth ... 2 Sam. 22:8-9 NKJ

8) So the Lord God said to the serpent, "Because you have done this, you will be punished. You ae singled out from all the domestic and wild animals of the whole earth to be cursed. You will grovel in the dust as long as you live, crawling along on your belly..." Gen. 3:14 NLT
Those who dwell in the wilderness will bow before Him, and His enemies will lick the dust. Ps. 72:9 NKJ

9) "...From now on, you and the woman will be enemies, and your offspring and her offspring will be enemies. ..." Gen.3:15 NLT

10) He will crush your head, and you will strike his heel." Gen. 3:15 NLT
He laid hold of the dragon, that serpent of old, who is the Devil and Satan ... and bound him ... and cast him into the bottomless pit ... Rv.20:2 NKJ

11) "... And though your desire will be for your husband, he will be your master"." Gen. 3:16 NKJ

12) "... cursed is the ground for thy sake; in sorrow shalt thou eat of it all the days of thy life; ... Gen.3:17 KJ

13) "In the sweat of thy face shalt thou eat bread until thou return unto the ground, for out of it wast thou taken: for dust thou art and unto dust thou shalt return."Gen. 3:19 KJ

14) The fear of you and the dread of you shall be on every beast of the earth, on every bird of the air, on all that move on the earth, and on all the fish of the sea. ... Every moving thing that lives shall be food for you. Gen. 9:2, 3 NKJ

15) When Adam sinned, sin entered the entire human race. Adam's sin brought death, so death spread to everyone, for everyone sinned. ... The sin of one man, Adam, caused death to rule over us ... Rom. 5:12, 17 NLT

16) ... for by whom a person is overcome, by him also he is brought into bondage. 2 Pet. 2:19 NKJ

CHAPTER 18. HOPE

1) Be silent in the presence of the Lord God; for the day of the Lord is at hand, for the Lord has prepared a sacrifice ... Zeph. 1:7 NKJ

2) For as in Adam all die, even so in Christ all shall be made alive. 1 Cor. 15:22 NKJ
   But when the fullness of the time had come, God sent forth His Son, born of a woman ... Gal. 4:4 NKJ

3) And it was not Adam who was fooled by Satan, but Eve, and sin was the result. 1 Tim. 2:14 LB

4) "If you want to be My follower you must love Me more than your own father and mother, wife and children, brothers and sisters - yes more than your own life. ..." (Jesus) Luke 14:26 NLT
   Then Peter began to say to Him, "See, we have left all and followed You." So Jesus answered... "there is no one who has left house, or (family), or wife or children ... for My sake ... who shall not receive a hundredfold now in this time - houses and (family) and lands, ...and eternal life... Mark 10:28-30 NKJ
   "...But Lord, what about this man?" ... Jesus said to him ... "what is that to you? You follow Me." John 21:21, 22 NKJ

5) Our God is the God of salvation. And to God the Lord belongs escapes from death. Ps. 68: 20 NKJ
   "... I have no pleasure in the death of one who dies," says the Lord God. Eze. 18:32 NKJ

6) Also for Adam and his wife, the Lord God made tunics of skin and clothed them. Gen. 3:21 NKJ

7) "I am the Lord, I am the Lord, the merciful and gracious God. I am slow to anger and rich in unfailing love and faithfulness. I show this unfailing love to many thousands by forgiving every kind of sin or rebellion. Even so I do not leave sin unpunished ,.. Ex. 34:6-7 NLT

8) And Adam was not deceived, but the woman being deceived, fell into transgression. 1Tim. 2:14 NKJ
   "... for I should have denied the God that is above ... If I covered my transgression as Adam (did) by hiding my iniquity in my bosom: ... Job 31:28, 33 KJ

Wherefore, as by one man sin entered into the world, and death by sin, ... Rom. 5:12 KJ

9) And Adam called his wife's name Eve; because she was the mother of all living. Gen. 3: 20 KJ
"Eve": from Hebrew word "*chayah*" meaning «to live». Primary root "to live, revive - keep alive", give life, to quicken, recover, repair, restore (to life), revive - save, be whole; life. Hebrew and Chaldee Dictionary, Strong's Exhaustive Concordance of the Bible. 2421. P. 39

CHAPTER 19. THE PLAN

1) Long ago, even before He made the world, God loved us and chose us ... His unchanging plan has always been to adopt us into his own family by bringing us to Himself through Jesus Christ. And this gave him great pleasure.
Eph. 1: 4,5 NLT
"Before I formed you in the womb I knew you: Before you were born I sanctified you; ..." Jer. 1:5 NKJ
... for God is love ... 1 John 4:8 LB

2) ... He will destroy ... The surface of the covering (that had been) cast over all people. And the veil that is spread over all nations ... Is. 25: 7, 8 NKJ
But their minds were blinded. For until this day, the same veil remains unlifted in the reading of the Old Testament, because the veil is taken away in Christ ... Nevertheless, when one turns to the Lord, the veil is taken away in Christ. 2 Cor. 3:14, 16 NKJ
... behold, the skin of (Moses's) face shone, and they were afraid to come near him... And when Moses had finished speaking with them, he put a veil on his face.
Ex. 34:30, 33 NKJ
...The veil shall be a divider for you between the holy place and the Most Holy. Ex. 26:33 NKJ

3) Then the Lord God said, "Behold, the man has become like one of Us, to know good and evil. And now, lest he put out his hand and take also of the tree of life, and eat and live forever ..." Gen. 3:22 NKJ

4) So He drove out the man; and placed cherubim at the east of the garden of Eden and a flaming sword ... to guard the way to the tree of life. Gen. 3:24 NKJ

5) ...because although they knew God, they did not glorify Him...but became futile in their thoughts, and their foolish hearts were darkened ... therefore God also gave them up ... Rom. 1:21, 24 NKJ
...Hearing you will hear and shall not understand, and seeing you will see and not perceive ... Matt. 13:14 NKJ

6) "In My Father's house are many mansions, ..." (Jesus Christ) John 14:2 NKJ

7) When Adam sinned, sin entered the entire human race. His sin spread death throughout all the world, so everything began to grow old ... Rom. 5:12 LB
Therefore the land will mourn; and everyone who dwells there will waste away with the beasts of the field and the birds of the air. Even the fish of the sea will be taken away. Hosea 4:3 NKJ
For we know that even the things of nature, like animals and plants, suffer in sickness and death ... Rom. 8:22 LB

8) For all creation is waiting patiently and hopefully for that future day when God will resurrect His children. For on that day thorns, and thistles, sin, death, and decay – the things that overcame the world against its will ... will all disappear....and the world around us ... will share in the glorious freedom from sin ... Rom. 8:20 LB

9) Jesus ... said to him, "Most assuredly I say to you, unless one is born again, he cannot see the kingdom of God." John 3:3 NKJ

10) Give no regard to mediums and familiar spirits; do not seek after them, to be defiled by them. I am the Lord your God. ... Lev. 20:6 NKJ
And the person who turns to mediums and familiar spirits, to prostitute himself with them, I will set My face against that person and cut him off from his people. Lev. 19:31 NKJ
Then said Saul unto his servants, Seek me a woman that hath a familiar spirit, ...Then said the woman, Whom shall I bring up unto thee? And he said, Bring me up Samuel.

And when the woman saw Samuel, she cried with a loud voice: .... 1 Sam.28:7, 11, 12 KJ

And when they shall say unto you, Seek unto them that have familiar spirits, and unto wizards that peep, and that mutter; should not a people seek unto their God? ... Is. 8:19 KJ

A man or woman who is a medium, or who has familiar spirits, shall surely be put to death, ...Lev. 20:27 NKJ

11) O Lord, I know it is not within the power of man to map his life and plan his course ... Jer. 10:23 LB

12) Now to Him who is able to do exceedingly abundantly above all that we ask or think ... be glory ... Eph. 3:20 NKJ

13) ... He began to be sorrowful and deeply distressed. Matt. 26:37 NKJ

14) Set me as a seal upon your heart ... For love is as strong as death, Jealousy as cruel as the grave, Its flames are flames of fire, A most vehement flame. Song 8:6 NKJ

15) "... let me clearly state to you and to all the people ... that it (the healing of a cripple) was done in the name and power of Jesus from Nazareth, the Messiah, the man you crucified—but God raised back to life again. ... There is salvation in no one else! Under all heaven there is no other name for men to call upon to save them." Acts 4:10, 12 LB

16) ... thorns and thistles, sin, death, and decay—the things that overcame the world against its will...will all disappear ... and the world around us will share [again] in the glorious freedom from sin which God's children enjoy. Rom. 8:20 LB

17) "Men can only reproduce human life, but the Holy Spirit gives new life from heaven, so don't be surprised at My statement that you must be born again!" John 3:6, 7 LB

18) ... When He roars, then His sons shall come ... Hosea 11: 10 NKJ

... the sheep hear his voice, and he calls his own sheep by name and leads them out...and the sheep follow him for they know his voice. Yet they will by no means follow a stranger ... John 10:3-5 NKJ

My sheep hear My voice, and I know them, and they follow Me. John 10:27 NKJ

CHAPTER 20. AFTERMATH

1) But now, thus says the Lord, who created you ... And He formed you ... I have called you by your name; You are Mine. Is. 43:1 NKJ

2) "... God Himself shall be with them and be their God. And God will wipe away every tear from their eyes, there shall be no more death, nor sorrow, nor crying. There shall be no more pain, for the former things have passed away." Rv. 21:3, 4 NKJ

3) For your Maker is your husband, the Lord of Hosts is His name. For the Lord has called you. My kindness shall not depart from you, nor My covenant of peace be removed. And every tongue which arises against you in judgement, you shall correctly judge and correct. Is. 54: 5, 10, 17 NKJ For I am jealous over you with godly jealousy; for I have espoused you to one husband, that I may present you as a chaste virgin to Christ. 2 Cor. 11:2

4) Casting down imaginations and every high thing that exalteth itself against the knowledge of God, and bringing into captivity every thought to the obedience of Christ. 2 Cor. 10: 5 KJ

5) I will lie down in peace and sleep, though I am alone, O Lord, You will keep me safe. Ps. 4:8 NKJ
"...When deep sleep falls upon men, while slumbering on their beds, then He opens the ears of men, and seals their instruction." Job 33:15 NKJ

www.ingramcontent.com/pod-product-compliance
Lightning Source LLC
Chambersburg PA
CBHW051133260626
47170CB00005B/1799